A Shot in the Dark

✪ ✪ ✪

"Please," he heard Father Dominic's pleading voice. "You cannot take the chalice and the cross. They are sacred relics, given to the service of God by the King of Spain more than two hundred years ago. Ten Abbots before me have kept them safe. I will not be the one who loses them. You will have to kill me first."

"Well, hell, preacher man, that ain't no problem," Purdone said, cocking his pistol.

"Hold it!" Sam shouted. He was still outside the chapel, but he had no choice. Purdone was about to kill Father Dominic.

"What the hell! Where did he come from?" Babbit shouted, snuffing out the one flickering candle. Outside, lit by the brightness of the moon, Sam was visible. Both Babbit and Purdone fired.

Sam felt a hammer-blow to his shoulder. He returned fire, heard someone groan then fall. A moment later, everything went black . . .

Also by Dale Colter

The Regulator
Diablo at Daybreak
Deadly Justice
Dead Man's Ride
Gravedancer
The Scalp Hunters
Paradise Mountain
Desert Pursuit
Montana Showdown

Published by
HARPERPAPERBACKS

THE REGULATOR

PAYBACK

DALE COLTER

HarperPaperbacks
A Division of HarperCollins*Publishers*

HarperPaperbacks *A Division of* HarperCollins*Publishers*
10 East 53rd Street, New York, N.Y. 10022

Cover illustration by Miro

First printing: September 1993

Printed in the United States of America

❖ 10 9 8 7 6 5 4 3 2 1

✪ PROLOGUE ✪

AS THE STAGECOACH CAME DOWN OUT OF the high country and began rolling across the flats, the six-horse team broke into an easy lope. The wheels of the swiftly moving stage kicked up a billowing trail of dust to roll and swirl on the road behind them, though a goodly amount of dust also managed to find its way into the passenger compartment.

"Oh, this dust," a woman complained. "It's intolerable. I don't know how anyone can live out here. Why, I can't even get my breath. George, do something."

"Now, Millie, be reasonable," the man

named George said. "What do you think I can do?"

"You could tell the driver to slow down. Perhaps if we wouldn't go so fast, the dust wouldn't be so bad."

"And we would be so far behind schedule that we would never get there," George replied. "No, even if I told him to slow down, I'm sure he wouldn't do so. You'll just have to find some way to tolerate it."

The woman was traveling with her husband and two small children. They were from Lexington, Kentucky, but were coming west because the husband had accepted a position in a bank.

There was only one other passenger in the coach. She was eighteen, pretty, and Indian, though she was wearing a dress that was decidedly non-Indian. She took a handkerchief from her handbag, held it under the spigot of the water barrel, and wet it. She wrung it out so that it wasn't dripping, then handed it to Millie.

"This will help," she said. "Hold it over your mouth and nose. The damp cloth will filter out some of the dust."

The woman took the handkerchief and did as the young woman suggested. A moment later she took it down and smiled at her.

"Why, that works marvelously," she said. "Thank you, my dear. But here, you take your handkerchief back. I'm sure you will have need for it. I will use my own."

"It doesn't bother me as much," the young woman said. "I'm used to it." She laughed. "Although I'm somewhat less used to it now than I was. I've been away for two years and I'm just coming back."

"Are you an Indian?" one of the little boys asked.

"Johnny!" the mother scolded.

The girl laughed, a soft, lilting laugh like the music of wind chimes.

"That's all right," she said. She looked at Johnny. "Yes, Johnny, I am Indian. I am Apache."

"Apache? They're the worst!" Johnny said.

"Johnny!" Millie gasped.

Again the girl laughed.

"I agree, my people are fierce warriors when provoked," she said. "But we can be very loyal friends." She extended her hand. "My name is Sasha. And now that I have told you my name, you and I must be friends, for the Apache people do not share their names easily."

"My, how interesting," Millie said. "You said you were away for two years. Where have you been?"

"I was selected from the mission school on the reservation to attend an Indian school in the East. I have been in Pennsylvania."

"Oh, how exciting for you."

"Yes, it was," Sasha agreed. "And I saw many wonderful things while I was there. Once, I even got to go to Washington to see the Capitol. But I must confess that I am very glad to be coming home again."

"Yes, well, I suppose there's nothing like home, even a place like this," Millie said. She looked through the window of the stage at the vast scenery sliding by outside. "And I must confess, it is beautiful out here in a rugged sort of way." She shivered. "But it is frightening, too. It's so big that it overwhelms you."

"Yes," Sasha agreed. "I think I didn't have any idea of the vastness of the territory out here until I saw the way things were in the East."

"What did you learn, Sasha?" George asked.

"I learned that people are people," Sasha said. "Whether they be Indian or white. And I learned that if we live together in peace, we can forge a wonderful future for everyone."

"Have you ever scalped anyone, Sasha?" Johnny asked.

"Johnny!" Millie said, her voice showing the level of her exasperation.

"No, I'm afraid not," Sasha replied, laughing easily. "Does that disappoint you, Johnny?"

Suddenly there was the sound of gunfire outside, and the coach rumbled to an unscheduled halt.

"What is it?" Millie asked in fear. "George, what's going on?"

"I don't know," George answered, looking out the window, as frightened as his wife.

"Sasha, do you have any idea?" Millie turned toward her new friend.

"No," Sasha replied. "Maybe someone is just signalling the driver to stop."

They heard loud angry voices outside, but at first they couldn't understand what was being said. Then, suddenly, a rider appeared just outside the stage. He was wearing a handkerchief tied across the bottom half of his face.

"You folks in the coach," he shouted in a loud, gruff voice. "Come on out of there!"

Cautiously George opened the door and stepped out onto the ground. Then he turned and helped his wife down, then the two children. Sasha was the last one to get out.

"What is this?" George demanded. "What's going on here?"

Millie looked up toward the driver and saw that he was tending to the shotgun guard. The guard's head was tilted back and his eyes were closed. His face was ashen, and that was when she saw that the front of his shirt was soaked with blood.

"George, that man has been shot."

"That he has, ma'am," one of the two riders said. "I shot 'im." He held up a canvas bag. "I shot 'im for this here money pouch. And now I'll be troublin' you folks for whatever money you have." The outlaw got down from his horse and walked over to them. His eyes were half-covered by droopy lids, one of which was puffed up with a scar the bandanna covering most of his face couldn't quite hide.

"I . . . I have no money," George said.

The scarred outlaw laughed. "Who you tryin' to kid, mister? The way you and your missus and them youngun's are all duded up there, why, I wouldn't be surprised if you wasn't carryin' more money on you than there is in this here pouch. Now, you can give it to me yourself, or I'll kill you an' take it off your body. Which is it to be?" The man cocked his pistol and pointed it at George.

"George, give it to him!" Millie insisted.

"It's all we have to live on until we get settled," George insisted.

"You're going to Gunther to take a job," Millie said. "We'll get by until you are paid. Give him the money!"

"You better listen to your wife, mister."

With a reluctant sigh, George took his billfold out and handed it over.

"There now, that's a good boy." The outlaw looked at Sasha. "And what about you?"

"I have no money," Sasha said.

"How did you buy a ticket with no money?"

"The Indian school where I attended classes provided me with a travel voucher," she said. "That was good for a ticket and meals until I returned home."

"The Injun school?" The rider looked at her more closely. "By God, you *are* a Injun, aren't you? Look at you, all dressed up like a white woman. And damn near as pretty, too, I'd say."

"Come on, Lucas, we got the pouch and the dude's poke. Let's get out of here."

"Lucas?" Sasha asked. "Would that be Lucas Babbit? I remember you from before I left."

Babbit sighed and pulled his handkerchief down. "Purdone, you got one hell of a big mouth, you know that?" he said. "And you, girl, you know too damn much." He cocked his pistol and pointed it at her.

"No!" Millie screamed. "Don't do it!"

"Can you give me one good reason why I shouldn't?" Babbit growled.

"Hell, I can," Purdone said.

Babbit looked up at him. "What?"

Purdone rubbed himself. "How long's it been since you had a soft Injun girl to lay with, Lucas?" he asked. "Seems to me like shootin' her would be a awful waste."

"I don't know," Babbit said. He smiled evilly at Sasha. "What do you think, girl? You think you could be nice to my partner an' me if we let you live?"

"I'd rather you shoot me," Sasha replied coldly.

"You would, huh? Purdone, drop me down that rope. We'll just tie this little ol' gal up an' take her with us."

"You have no right to do that!" George said angrily.

Babbit growled. "Right? Mister, I got the right to do anything I want, long as I've got this," he said.

"But she's just a young girl, an innocent child," George insisted.

Babbit laughed. "Mister, there ain't no one innocent."

Purdone tossed down the rope and Babbit looped it around Sasha, then started to tie her up with it. With his attention diverted, George thought he saw the opportunity to jump him, and he did, knocking the outlaw down by the surprise of his action. Emboldened by his initial success, George reached down to grab Babbit and administer another blow when Babbit's arm suddenly thrust up. George let out an expulsion of air as if he had been hit in the solar plexus. He backed away from Babbit, clutching his stomach. He looked over at his wife with a surprised expression on his face.

"Millie?" he said in a small voice.

At first Millie didn't quite know what happened. Then she saw the bloodstained knife in Babbit's hand.

"No!" she screamed. "No!" She rushed to her husband, who by now had fallen to the ground.

"Papa!" the two boys cried.

Millie cushioned George's head in her lap while he breathed his last gasps.

"Millie, I . . ." he started, then he sighed and was still.

"My God!" Millie said, looking up at Babbit. "You've killed him!"

"Yeah, lady, it happens to all of us sometime," Babbit said coldly. "But I reckon I can send you to him if you want." He pointed his pistol at her and cocked it.

"No!" Sasha shouted. "No, don't hurt her! Don't hurt anyone else!"

Babbit lowered the hammer and looked at her. "You'll go with us without no trouble?"

"Yes," she said. "Yes, I'll go without giving you any trouble."

"What's she goin' to ride?" Purdone asked. "We only got two horses."

"Ride?" Babbit replied. "Hell, she ain't *goin'* to ride. She's Injun, ain't she? She can run alongside us. We won't go too fast for her to keep up, and if we do, why, we'll just drag her."

Holding his end of the rope, Babbit remounted, then, giving Sasha a jerk, started riding. Half stumbling and half running, Sasha managed to keep up with them as they rode away. Once, she looked back over her shoulder at the stagecoach, standing still on the road behind her. The driver was looking at the guard, who Sasha now knew was dead, while Millie and the two boys were gathered around George's body on the ground. Lost in their own sorrow, they didn't even bother to look up as she was led away.

THE METAL BIT JANGLED AGAINST THE horse's teeth. The horse's hooves clattered on the hard rock and the leather saddle creaked beneath the weight of its rider. The rider was a tall man, with ice-blue eyes and a scar that ran like a purple flash of lightning from his left sideburn down to the corner of his thin-lipped mouth.

Sam Slater's boots were dusty and well-worn; the metal of his spurs had become dull with time. He wore a Colt .44 at his hip and carried a Winchester .44-40 in his saddle sheath.

He dismounted, unhooked his canteen, and took a swallow, then poured some water into his hat. He held it in front of his horse. The horse drank thirstily, though Sam knew that the small amount of water did little to slake the animal's thirst. The horse drank all the water then began nuzzling Sam for more.

"Sorry," Sam said quietly. "But that's the best I can do for now. But we'll reach the monastery before nightfall, and there will be water there."

The monastery Sam referred to stood alone in the desert, a testament to the faith that God would provide for the righteous, even in conditions as harsh as this. Records in the monastery indicated that it had been built by the Spanish nearly two hundred years earlier. There were no natural sources of food or water. The monastery garden was supported by irrigation, the water for which was carried in by barrel from a small, not always dependable river, twelve miles to the east.

Except for the members of the religious order who lived in the monastery, no one—Indian, Mexican, or American—lived within fifty miles of the place. As far as anyone could tell, no one had ever lived here. The question then was why had it been built here, and why did the religious order continue to occupy it?

Sam Slater had posed that same question to

Father Dominic when he was here once before. With a small smile, Father Dominic had replied: "The answer is a mystery, and the mystery is the answer."

Slater had come to the conclusion yesterday morning that Babbit and Purdone were headed for the monastery. It shouldn't have come as a surprise to him. Anyone coming this way would have to stop at the monastery, for there was no other source of food or water within several miles in any direction.

Babbit and Purdone were desperate fugitives, men whose faces were plastered on wanted bills all across the Southwest. They were wanted for murder and robbery, having held up several stagecoaches and, in the process, killing a couple of guards. The money offered for their capture was five hundred dollars each.

Finding wanted men and turning them over to the law for a reward was Sam Slater's business. Such men were known as bounty hunters, or regulators. Sam was particularly good at his job . . . so good in fact that men often spoke generally of regulators, but when they spoke specifically of *the* Regulator, everyone knew they were speaking only of Sam Slater.

In the case of Babbit and Purdone, however, the chase had gone beyond business. It became personal for Sam when, three days ago, he had come across Sasha's body.

Sam knew the girl and her parents, for they were from the same village where Sam had once lived. Despite that, he almost didn't recognize her when he found her. Her nude body was blackened and swollen in the sun. She had stab wounds all over her body and one of her breasts had been hacked away. It was as brutal and senseless a murder as Sam had ever encountered, and from that point on, the reward money became secondary.

Just before dark Sam reached the monastery, which was surrounded by high stone walls and secured by a heavy oak gate. When he pulled on a rope attached to a short section of log, the makeshift knocker banged against the large, heavy gates with a booming thunder that resonated through the entire monastery. A moment later a small window slid open and a brown-hooded face appeared in the opening.

"Who are you?" the face asked.

"My name is Sam."

"What do you want?"

"I want to come in."

"I'm sorry. We can grant no entry."

"But, Brother, I am out of water. You cannot turn me away."

"I am truly sorry," the monk said. "God go with you." The little window slammed shut.

Sam had been here many times before, and he had never been denied entry. In fact, he knew the gatekeeper personally, a man named Brother Tobias. Brother Tobias had a weakness for lemon-drop candy and Sam sometimes brought some to him. He knew then that from the very beginning of their conversation, when Brother Tobias asked who he was, something was wrong. Brother Tobias was trying to send Sam a message.

Sam got on his horse and rode away from the gate.

Lucas Babbit and Justin Purdone were standing just inside the gate. Purdone was peering through the crack between the timbers of the gate.

"What's he doin'?" Babbit asked.

"He's ridin' off," Purdone answered.

Babbit chuckled, then put his pistol away. He looked at the short, overweight monk. "You done that real good, padre," he said. "I don't think he suspects a thing."

"I am not a priest," Brother Tobias said. "Therefore I am not addressed as Father."

"Yeah, well, brother, sister, father, padre, reverend, pastor, what the hell difference does it make? All you religious guys are called somethin'. Come on, let's go see if the cook has our supper finished. I'm starvin'."

The three men walked back across the little courtyard, which, because of the irrigation and loving care bestowed upon it by the brothers of the order, was lush with flowers, fruit trees, and a vegetable garden. There were a dozen or more monks in the yard, each one occupied in some specific task.

The building they entered was surprisingly cool, kept that way by the hanging ollas, which, while sacrificing some of the precious water by evaporation, paid off the investment by lowering the temperature by several degrees.

"Who was at the gate?" Father Dominic asked.

"A stranger, Father. I do not know who he was," Brother Tobias said.

"And you denied him sanctuary?"

"I had no choice, Father," Brother Tobias said, rolling his eyes toward Babbit and Purdone.

"You sent him away?" Father Dominic asked Babbit.

Babbit was a big, ugly man, with yellow eyes, a drooping eyelid, and a puffy scar passing through the eyelid and coming to a hook under his nose.

Purdone was much smaller, with a ferretlike face and skin, heavily pocked from the scars of some childhood disease.

"He wasn't no ordinary visitor," Babbit said. "His name was Sam Slater, a fella they call the Regulator. He's not exactly someone we would want around right now."

"I see," Father Dominic said. "Still, to turn someone away is unthinkable. It is a show of Christian kindness to offer water, food, and shelter to those who ask it of us."

"You're showin' your Christian kindness by takin' care of us," Babbit said. "Now, what about that food? How long does it take your cook to fix a little supper?"

"Forgive me for not mentioning it the moment you came in," Father Dominic said. "The cook has informed me that your supper is ready."

"Well, now, that's more like it! Why didn't you say somethin'?" Babbit growled. "Come on, Justin. Let's get somethin' to eat."

"What is this?" Babbit asked a moment later, when a bowl of beans and a plate of tortillas were set on the table before them.

"This is your supper."

"Is this it? What about that Christian kindness you were talkin' about? You didn't offer us no meat?" Babbit growled.

Father Dominic shook his head. "I'm sorry, in this order we do not eat meat. This is our regular fare. We cannot offer you what we do not have."

"It ain't that bad, Lucas," Purdone said, rolling up a tortilla in his fingers and filling it with beans. "It ain't bad at all, and it sure beats jerky."

* * *

Sam waited until after dark before he returned to the monastery. Leaving his horse hobbled, he slipped up to one of the side walls, then, using chinks and holes in the stone facade to provide foot- and hand-holds, he climbed up, slipped over the top, then dropped to the ground on the inside.

Most of the buildings inside the monastery grounds were dark, for candles and oil for lamps were precious commodities to be used sparingly, though here and there a flickering light managed to escape. It wasn't totally dark, however, for the moon was full and bright, and the chapel, dormitory, stable, storage, and grain buildings all gleamed in a soft, silver light like white blooms, sprouting from desert cactus.

The night was alive with the long, high-pitched trills and low violalike thrums of the frogs. For counterpoint there were crickets, the long, mournful howl of coyotes, and from the stable, a mule braying and a horse whickering.

With his gun in hand, and staying in the shadows alongside the wall, Sam moved toward the chapel. He found a window and looked inside. There, he saw Babbit, Purdone, and Father Dominic. Babbit and Purdone were pointing their pistols at Father Dominic, who was clutching a chalice and cross tightly to his chest.

"Please." He heard Father Dominic's pleading voice. "You cannot take the chalice and the cross. They are sacred relics, given to the service of God by the King of Spain more than two hundred years ago. Ten abbots before me have kept them safe. I will not be the one who loses them."

"They're gold, ain't they?" Babbit asked.

"Yes."

"Then I'm takin' 'em."

"You will have to kill me first," Father Dominic insisted.

"Well, hell, preacher man, that ain't no problem," Purdone said, cocking his pistol.

"Hold it!" Sam shouted. He was still outside the chapel, looking through the window, certainly not in the position he wanted to be to challenge them. But he had no choice. Purdone was about to kill Father Dominic.

"What the hell! Where did he come from?" Babbit shouted. Babbit was standing by the one flickering candle, and he snuffed it out. The inside of the chapel was immediately plunged into darkness. Because of that, Sam couldn't see anyone inside. Because he was outside, and lighted by the brightness of the moon, however, he was visible, and both Babbit and Purdone fired.

Sam felt a hammer-blow to his shoulder. He returned fire, using the flame pattern from inside as his target. He heard someone groan, then fall. A moment later he heard a crash of glass from the other side of the building and he realized that someone had jumped through the window. He hurried around to try to head him off, but, to his surprise, suddenly found himself growing very dizzy. After that, everything went black.

Lucas Babbit was the one who had leaped through the window and escaped into the night. Luckily for Sam, Babbit didn't know that Sam had been wounded and was, even then, lying passed out just behind the chapel. Had Babbit known that, he would have finished the job.

Justin Purdone was the man Sam shot in the exchange of gunfire that night, and he died before morning. Even though he was an outlaw who had bullied the brothers and was in the process of stealing their most precious artifacts, they prayed over his body and buried him, if not in the consecrated graveyard, at least on the grounds.

It was two weeks before Sam left the monastery, his shoulder patched and now nearly mended, thanks to the nursing skills of the brothers of the order. He was leaving empty-handed, for not only had Babbit gotten away, but Sam had no proof that the man he had killed in the shoot-out was Justin Purdone. And without proof, there would be no reward.

Sam was pretty easy about it. As far as he was concerned, it wasn't a total loss. Purdone had been one of those responsible for killing Sasha Quiet Stream and he was now dead. And though Babbit was on the loose, he was still out there, and Sam was mended and on the prowl again. He had no doubt but that he would cross paths with Babbit again someday. In the meantime, there were other outlaws with prices on their head, and Sam wasn't the kind to let his business come to a stop because of one little setback.

One year later

THE TERRIBLE PAIN STOPPED AND A WARMING numbness set in. It was the numbness that allowed Ray Barnett to keep up with the others on their mad ride away from the holdup. But with the numbness there also came a weakness from loss of blood, and by the time they rode into the little town of Braggadocio just before dawn the next morning, Barnett was staying in his saddle only by supreme effort of will.

"Hey, Charley, Ray's about to keel over here," Billy Purcell said. Purcell had taken it on himself to ride beside Barnett, and for the last three hours had held the reins of Barnett's horse while Barnett used both hands on the pommel just to stay up.

"Stay with him," Charley ordered. Charley Harris was the leader of the gang; on the afternoon of the day before, they had hit the bank in Gunther for five thousand dollars.

"Maybe we can find a doctor in town to fix him up," Purcell suggested.

"We don't have time," Charley growled. "That posse's goin' to be on us like stink on shit if we wait around here."

"He can't go on much longer, Charley. He needs a doctor."

"He's gut-shot, ain't he? He's goin' to die anyway. Takin' him to a doctor just to have him tell us Barnett is goin' to croak is goin' to slow us down more."

"You're all heart, Charley," Barnett grunted.

"Yeah, well, we could just drop you off by the side of the road," Charley explained.

"That's a good idea. Why don't we do that?" Sims asked.

"But look, we got to eat, ain't we?" Purcell suggested. "Maybe we could have the doc's woman fix us some hot grub while he's lookin' at Ray."

"Yeah, all right," Charley agreed. "We'll stop, but just for long enough to get somethin' to eat."

It was still predawn dark, but as the four men rode through the street, their way was lighted by squares of golden light on the ground, cast through the windows of the houses where early risers were already beginning to set to breakfast.

Charley halted his men when they reached the end of the street.

"What is it?" Purcell asked.

"You wanted to take him to the doc, didn't you? Well, that's the doc's house down there," Charley said.

"How do you know?"

"I was here once. You know, as I think back on it, the doc's got him a fine-lookin' woman, too. Don't know how an old fool like him got such a young, pretty wife. I seen 'er the first time, I thought she was his daughter."

The house Charley pointed to was a low, single-story building that stood nearly half a block away from the others. A wisp of wood smoke rose from the chimney, carrying with it the aroma of frying bacon.

"Before we ride up there, fellas, take a good look around," Charley said. "Make sure nobody is watchin' us."

The saddles squeaked as the riders twisted to look around. Barnett held on, telling himself there was only a short time left, then he could lie down and rest in a nice, soft, bed.

"It looks clear," one of the men said.

"Let's go," Charley replied. He clicked to his horse and the four of them moved slowly across the distance. They stopped just in front of the doctor's house.

BURL PRESNELL, M.D., the sign read by the door. Charley didn't bother to knock, he just pushed it open. Kelly Sims and Billy Purcell half carried, half supported Barnett inside.

"What the . . . what is this?" the surprised doctor asked, looking up from his breakfast table. His wife was standing at the stove frying bacon, and she looked around in alarm as well.

"Don't get fretted none, doc," Charley said. "I'm Charley Harris. I reckon you've heard of me."

"Cactus Charley!" Dr. Presnell gasped. "Yes, yes, of course I've heard of you."

Though only twenty-one years old, Charley Harris had already achieved a degree of notoriety as a result of his lawless rampage. His picture decorated wanted posters all over the Southwest, and of late, as "Cactus Charley," he had been glamorized as the subject of half a dozen dime novels.

Charley grinned broadly. "Yeah, Cactus Charley, that's me," he said. He was proud of his notoriety, and even though he could barely read, he had a copy of each of the novels that had been written about him. "One of my men got hisself pretty bad shot yesterday afternoon. He needs some doctorin'." He looked over toward the stove. "And the rest of us need some grub."

"What makes you think I would—" Dr. Presnell started, then he stopped and sighed. "Never mind, bring him in. Let me take a look at him."

Purcell and Sims lay Barnett on the bed. Dr. Presnell sat beside him, then opened his shirt.

"He's lucky," he said. "I don't think there's any festering. But the bullet is going to have to come out."

"Hell, why bother?" Charley asked. "He's gut-shot. That means he's goin' to die."

"Probably," Dr. Presnell said. "But not absolutely. I can at least try."

"You want to waste your time on him, go right ahead. Me, I want somethin' to eat. Miz?"

"There's bacon and a skillet," the doctor's wife said. "And a basket of fresh eggs. There's also a pan of biscuits, fresh made. If you want breakfast, fix it yourself. I have to help my husband tend to this man's wound."

Charley pulled his pistol and pointed it at Barnett. "Well, hell, if that's all that's gettin' in the way of us gettin' a little grub, I can just put him out of his misery now."

Dr. Presnell stepped between Charley and Barnett. "If you shoot him, you're goin' to have to shoot me, too," he said.

"All right by me," Charley said easily.

"And me," the woman added, stepping in front of her husband.

Charley looked at them for a moment longer, then chuckled. "All right, have it your way. Billy, you fix the breakfast."

"Why me? I ain't no cook."

"I said fix the goddamn breakfast," Charley ordered, his voice flat and cold. "You the one wanted to get Ray tended to."

"All right, all right," Purcell mumbled.

"Doc, you not only got yourself a young, pretty woman, you got a brave one, too," Charley said. "How did an old fart like you get someone like that?"

When Dr. Presnell didn't answer, Charley gave both husband and wife an insolent smile and nod, then walked over to join the others at the kitchen stove.

"Here's a little laudanum," Dr. Presnell said to Barnett, handing him a small bottle. "Take it. You'll need it when I start probing for the bullet."

Dr. Presnell's wife assisted him. They removed Barnett's shirt and the doctor began digging in the wound for the bullet. Charley, Purcell, and Sims ate their breakfast as if totally unconcerned with what was going on over on the bed. A few minutes later Presnell announced that he had the bullet and he dropped it with a clink into the pan of warm water. The bullet lay in the bottom of the pan with tiny bubbles of blood rising to paint a swirl of red on the water's surface. No one at the breakfast table seemed particularly interested in the medical report.

"You 'bout finished over there, doc?" Charley asked, coming from table, carrying a sandwich made from bacon and a biscuit.

"I've got the bullet out."

"Good, get him patched up so we can put him back on his horse."

"This man can't go anywhere," Dr. Presnell said. "Why, if you take him out of here now, it'll kill him."

"He knew the chances, just like the rest of us," Charley said. "Ray," he said gruffly. "Come on, Ray. Get up!"

Barnett groaned.

"Why don't we leave him here, like the doc said?" Purcell asked.

"We can't do that. He knows where we're goin'. He might talk."

"Barnett won't talk," Purcell said. "He's a good man, he won't talk."

"We killed two people in that holdup," Charley said. "That means if we get caught, we're goin' to hang. If they tell him they won't hang him if he'll help 'em find us, are you tellin' me he won't talk?"

"Well, what are we goin' to do," Purcell

asked, "if we can't take him with us and we can't leave him here?"

Charley looked at Barnett, unconscious now, and sighed. "Shit!" he finally said. "There's only one thing we can do."

Charley walked over to the bed and picked up a pillow, then pushed it down over Barnett's face.

"What? What are you doing?" The doctor's wife gasped in shock. She reached for Charley, but he hit her in the face with a wicked backhand, which sent her careening backward where she hit the wall, then slid down into a sitting position.

"Stop!" Dr. Presnell said. "Stop, you're going to kill him!"

"Yeah, doc, that's what I aim to do," Charley answered with a giggle.

Barnett began to struggle beneath the pillow and Charley pressed it down harder.

"Charley, look out!" Sims suddenly called, and the outlaw looked over to see Dr. Presnell fumbling desperately with a shotgun, trying to close the breech.

Charley pulled his pistol and fired, his bullet hitting Presnell right between the eyes. The doctor's wife screamed and Charley turned toward her.

"Shut up!" he shouted. "Shut up!"

She screamed again.

Charley fired a second time and the woman quit screaming. A tiny black hole appeared just over her left breast. A trickle of blood oozed down from the hole and her head slumped back against the wall, her eyes open and sightless.

"Shit!" Charley said. "Now look what you made me do."

Outside, and all through the neighborhood, dogs began to bark.

"What was that?" a distant voice called.

"Charley, we better get outta here!" Purcell warned. "The whole town's done been woke up."

"What about Ray?" Purcell asked.

"I'll make sure he's dead," Sims replied.

"I think those shots come from the doc's house," someone shouted from outside.

"Never mind that! Come on!" Charley growled to Sims. "Leave him. We ain't got time to check. We got to get out of here."

At Charley's shouted command, the three outlaws bolted through the front door and onto their horses. With the sun showing streaks of red in the eastern sky, they galloped out of town past a dozen or more townspeople, who were, by then, hurrying down to the doctor's house to see the carnage that had been left behind.

Three weeks later

"You check the horses?" Charley asked as Purcell came walking back into camp. "They coulda got loose in that storm last night. I wouldn't want to be out here on foot."

"They didn't go nowhere," Purcell said. He sat down on a rock, picked up a stick, and began poking in the dirt. "Charley, how much longer we got to stay out here like this? What's the good of havin' all that money in our saddlebags if we can't spend none of it?"

"I figure that storm last night done us more good than about anythin'," Charley said. "It for sure wiped out our tracks so's no one could trail us. A week or two with no trail to speak of and things will die down," Charley said.

"If we hadn't killed that doctor and his wife, the whole damn territory wouldn't be lookin' for us," Purcell suggested.

"And if you hadn't insisted we get Ray a doctor, I wouldn'ta had to kill the doctor and his wife."

"He was hurtin' somethin' awful," Purcell said. "You wouldn't let a horse suffer like he was."

"You'd shoot a horse," Sims suggested.

"Yeah, well, we'da been better off shootin' Ray and leavin' him on the side of the trail somewhere," Charley suggested. He leaned over the fire and tested the meat he was roasting. "This here rabbit looks about done."

"This is a hell of a breakfast, ain't it? I'm gettin' damned tired of rabbit, and squirrel and prairie chicken and the like," Purcell growled. "I want a steak."

"And people in hell want ice water," Charley said. "Shut up your bitchin'. You don't want any rabbit, fine, me an' Sims will eat your part."

"Didn't say I wasn't goin' to eat it. Just said I was tired of it."

Charley took out his knife and started to cut off a piece of rabbit. Just as he did so, however, there was a loud popping sound, then the smack of a bullet crashing into the rabbit. Pieces of the cooked animal flew in every direction.

Charley let out a shout of fear and alarm and jumped back from his demolished breakfast. The other two men jumped up and pulled their guns.

"Just drop 'em right there," a voice called.

"What the hell? Who are you, mister? Show yourself!" Charley shouted.

There was another gunshot and this time the bullet hit the ground right between Charley's feet, then ricocheted up between his legs and whined out over the open prairie.

"I'll take off your balls with the next shot," the voice growled.

"No, no!" Charley said, dropping his gun and raising his hands. "We give up! We give up!"

Sims and Billy dropped their guns and raised their hands as well.

"That's more like it," the disembodied voice said. There was the sound of boots walking on rocky ground, then a man appeared from behind a rock. He was carrying three pairs of handcuffs and he tossed them forward. "How about you fellas trying these on for size?" he asked.

"Who the hell are you, mister? I don't see no badge," Purcell said.

Charley chuckled softly. "He don't need no badge. Boys, this here is the man they call the Regulator. That is you, ain't it? Sam Slater?"

"I'm Slater," Sam said.

"Time was, boys, when Slater was the best," Charley said. "'Course, that was before he run into Lucas Babbit. The way I hear it, he had Lucas cornered, but Lucas beat him in a shoot-out and got away. Is that the way it happened, Slater?" Charley taunted.

"Don't concern yourself with Lucas Babbit. You're the ones occupying my attention now."

"I'm flattered," Charley replied. "Boys," he said to the others. "We should be flattered. The Regulator only goes after the best."

"Not the best, sonny," Sam replied coldly. "Just the ones who pay the most. That business you pulled back in Braggadocio got the dander up in quite a few folks. You fellas are worth five hundred dollars apiece."

"Five hundred dollars apiece, eh?" Charley said. He smiled. "Well, now, I think we can beat that, don't you, boys? We'll give you two thousand to let us go."

Sam shook his head. "Not worth it," he said.

"What do you mean it's not worth it? That's five hundred more than you'll get for the three of us."

"I do somethin' like that, that'd make me an outlaw and I wouldn't be able to collect any more rewards for scum like you. Besides, it's goin' to be worth five hundred bucks to me just to watch the four of you hang."

"The four of us? What do you mean four of us?"

"Barnett's in jail back in Gunther."

"I'll be damned. I was sure the son of a bitch would be dead by now."

Slater took his rope and made three nooses. He put the nooses around the necks of each of his prisoners before ordering them to mount up. As Purcell started to get on his horse he slipped, causing a pull against the neck of the other two men.

"Careful there, you dumb bastard!" Charley growled. "You want to break all our necks?"

Once all three prisoners were mounted, Slater tied the end of the rope to his saddle, then he swung up onto his horse.

"Okay, gents," he said easily. "Let's head for Gunther."

SAM SLATER WATCHED THE DUST RISE FROM the hoof falls of his three prisoners and he thought about the fact that Lucas Babbit was still a free man. Charley Harris had taunted him about it, obviously trying to get a rise out of the bounty hunter. What Charley didn't realize was that he had come much closer than he expected, because the subject of Lucas Babbit was still a sensitive one as far as Sam was concerned.

Sam could not afford to give up everything else just to find Lucas Babbit, but the outlaw was never far from his mind. There was seldom a day that went by that he didn't think about

Babbit, and whenever he rode into a new town, he found that no matter who he was looking for, no matter what dodger he had in his hand, he was also always looking for a big man with yellow eyes, a drooping eyelid, and a puffed, ugly scar. Sam was tired. It wasn't just the butt-sore tiredness of a long, hard ride. It was the kind of bone-deep weariness that comes on a man after years of riding the trail with one dusty town behind his back and another just ahead.

The bad side of it was that it would never get any better.

The good side was that at this stage, it could get no worse.

The anchorless drifting had become a part of Sam's existence. He was a man who had been permanently marked by the saloons, cow towns, stables, dusty streets, and open prairies he had encountered. He could not deny them without denying his own life and, in fact, had no intention of ever doing so. He was both a long way from home and as close to home as the nearest hotel, or back room in a saloon, or even a whore's bed. Most often, though, home was no more than a bedroll made from a saddle blanket and poncho.

"Hey, Slater, you goin' to push us all night, or are we goin' to get a chance to rest a bit?" Charley asked.

"Keep goin'," Sam growled. "We'll be there by midnight."

"Midnight?" Charley complained. "What the hell? You jumped us 'fore daylight this mornin'. You got no right to push us till midnight. I've heard tell that peace officers have to give their prisoners proper rest, food, an' water."

"Well, there you go, Charley, I'm not a peace officer," Sam said. "Besides, I wouldn't be worryin' a whole lot about rest if I was you. You and your compadres there will be getting an eternity of rest in just about a week or so."

"Yeah? Well, we'll see about that," Charley replied.

"Charley? Charley, you said if we teamed up with you, they'd never catch us," Sims said. "I don't want to hang, Charley. You hear me? I don't want to hang."

"Shut up, Kelly," Charley said. "Ain't nothin' to be gained by whimperin'."

"All of you keep quiet," Sam said. "I'm not in any mood to listen to your prattle."

"How 'bout if I sing a little song?" Charley started. "'Buffalo Gals, won't you come out tonight, come out tonight, come out—uhnn!'"

The sudden end to his song was brought on by Sam jerking hard on the rope. As the rope was looped around Charley's neck, it had the effect of choking off his efforts.

"Watch it!" Charley said. "You could jerk me off here an' break my neck!"

"Really? Well, I wouldn't want to do that,

now, would I, Charley?" Sam said. "That would spoil everyone's fun in watching you hang."

"I hate disappointin' all those nice folks like that, Slater," Charley said. "But I ain't plannin' on givin' them a show."

Despite their further protests, Sam Slater pushed his three prisoners far into the night, arriving in Gunther so late that three of the four saloons were already dark and the fourth, though still showing light from the bottom floor, was quiet. The four horses plodded down the dirt street, the hollow clopping echoing back from the darkened false-fronted stores and houses. From the back of one of the houses, a baby cried and Sam heard the cooing sound of its mother as she comforted it. Such sounds barely penetrated Sam's consciousness. He was aware that another world existed outside his own . . . a world of husbands and wives, children and homes, schools, churches, and socials, but such things were so remote from his own experience that he was unable even to dredge up a twinge of envy, or regret, for his exclusion.

The jail, like the other buildings in town, was dark. Sam stopped in front and swung down from his horse.

"Ha!" Charley barked in what might have been a laugh. "The sheriff an' his deputies have all gone home for the night. You're goin' to have to bring us back tomorrow."

"You could take us over to the hotel, maybe rent us a room," Purcell suggested.

"Hotel, hell? How 'bout takin' us down to the saloon? We could prob'ly find some whores that'd share their bed with us tonight," Purcell said.

"Don't know 'bout Slater, though," Charley added. "What self-respectin' whore would have anythin' to do with him?"

Sam tied his horse off at the hitch rail, then stepped up onto the wooden porch in front of the jail. His boots clumped loudly across the boards. His horse whickered, and Sam spun around quickly, his pistol in his hand, the hammer pulled back. Just as he had suspected, the three were trying to ease out of the hitch.

"Hold it, hold it!" Charley said. "We ain't goin' nowhere!"

"Charley, that's just about the first true words you've spoken," Sam said. "You ain't goin' nowhere."

Keeping his pistol leveled at his three prisoners, Sam banged on the front door of the jail house.

"What do you want?" a muffled voice called from inside.

"Open the door. I've got some prisoners for you."

"Prisoners? We wasn't expectin' no prisoners. Who might they be?"

"Charley Harris, Kelly Sims, Billy Purcell," Sam answered.

"What the hell? You got them?" the voice called. Sam could hear footsteps from inside. A key rattled in the lock and a moment later the door opened. A man, obviously roused from his sleep, stood there, wearing boots and a pair of long johns. "Who are you?" he asked.

"Slater."

"Slater? Sam Slater? The fella they call the Regulator?"

"You going to take these prisoners or not?"

"Yes, yes, sir, I'll take them," the man said. "I'm Deputy Dave Carter, Mr. Slater. Boy, oh boy, is Sheriff McQuade goin' to be surprised come mornin'."

Carter reached up beside the door. When he pulled his hand back, it was clutched around a Greener ten-gauge shotgun. He pointed the double-barrel weapon at the three men.

"Okay, you boys, just climb on down real easy now," he said. "I've got a nice room all ready for you."

"These men are worth five hundred dollars each," Sam said. "I'll be needing you to sign a receipt."

"I can't give you no money, Mr. Slater. I'm just the deputy 'round here."

"That's all right," Sam said. "All you have to do is sign the receipt, stating that I brought them in. I'll take care of the rest."

"Yes, sir, I'll be proud to do that, soon as I get these critters locked up. Come along, boys. We got a friend of yours in there, already waitin' to hang. I reckon he can wait a little longer so's you can all hang together." He jabbed Charley in the ribs with the barrel of his shotgun.

"Hey, watch it. That hurts," Charley complained.

"Does it?" the deputy asked, jabbing him again. "Well, now, that's too bad."

Fifteen minutes later Sam was standing at the bar over in the Knucklebuster Saloon.

"Got any Old Overholt?" he asked when the bartender moved down to stand in front of him.

The bartender, who was sucking on a toothpick, nodded without speaking, then turned to pull a bottle down from the wall behind him. He poured a glass and slid it in front of Sam.

"You the fella brung them three in a while ago?" the bartender asked.

Sam nodded, then tossed the drink down.

"Seen you comin' in," the bartender said. "Me and Lily there was the only two down here an' we heard the horses, so we looked out to see who it was."

"Who was they?" Lily asked. Lantern light

was kind to Lily. Her skin glowed soft and golden and the dissipation of her life didn't show so badly. She managed to look almost as young as her years.

"Charley Harris, Kelly Sims, Billy Purcell," Sam said, pouring himself a second drink.

"You caught the rest of that bunch?" Lily asked. "All of 'em? All alone?" She walked down to stand beside him. "Karl, pour this man another drink, on me," she said. She smiled up at Sam. "It was bad enough them killin' that teller and poor Mr. Hancock when they robbed the bank here. But I heard what they done over in Braggadocio to poor Dr. Presnell and his wife. And the Presnells doin' no more than their Christian duty to succor the wounded. That's one hangin' I don't aim to miss."

Sam took the drink Karl poured, then, with his glass, saluted the woman who had bought it for him. The light was less kind up close, but there was still something appealing about her. Maybe it was the good humor in her eyes, still alive despite the brutality of her profession. Maybe it was the swell of her breasts, soft and inviting to a man, many weeks on the trail. Or maybe he was just bone-tired and needed someone to help him make it through the rest of the night.

"You got company for the night?" he asked.

Lily's smile deepened in practiced seductiveness. "Can't say as I do," she said.

"Want some?"

"Are you offerin'?"

"I'm offering."

"I'm acceptin'," she said, hooking her arm through his.

Six weeks later

"ALL RISE!"

There was a scrape of chairs and a rustle of pants, petticoats, and skirts as the spectators in the courtroom stood. A spittoon rang as one male member of the gallery made a last-second, accurate expectoration of his tobacco quid.

"Oyez, oyez, oyez. This court is now in session, the Honorable Amon Smiley presiding."

The gallery was limited to fifty spectators and tickets for attendance were highly prized commodities. Most people agreed that Judge

Smiley's performances were the best show anywhere, not because of any particular showmanship, but because of his hard-nosed treatment of criminals. He had sentenced so many hardened criminals to hang that he was known far and wide as "King of the Gallows."

Judge Smiley stepped through a rear door and viewed his court. He wasn't a tall man, but he was robust, with a square face and piercing blue eyes. He moved quickly to the bench, then sat down.

"Be seated," he said.

The gallery sat, then watched with interest as the convicted prisoners were brought into the room. Included in the gallery were several representatives from the nation's press. Newspapers from San Francisco to New York had capitalized on the notoriety of Cactus Charley, of dime-novel fame, and some of the stories openly treated him as a folk hero. Such stories concentrated on the derring-do of the bank robbery and escape, conveniently omitting the details of the murder of Dr. Presnell and his wife. The jury, however, composed of twelve hardened citizens of the frontier town of Gunther, was unimpressed by the gang's notoriety. They listened to testimony from witnesses to the bank robbery and from the citizens of Braggadocio, who reported hearing shots, seeing Charley Harris, Billy Purcell, and Kelly Sims ride away from the doctor's house, then finding the doctor and his wife dead and the fourth member of their gang, Ray Barnett, nearly so. Barnett had already been tried, convicted, and sentenced to be hanged for his part in the killing of the bank teller and Loren Hancock during the bank holdup. In a hollow victory, Barnett was found innocent of the deaths of Dr. Presnell and his wife.

The evidence was overwhelming and the jury returned a verdict of guilty on all counts. Now all that remained was for Judgc Smiley to pass on their sentence.

"Bailiff, would you position the prisoners before the bench for sentencing, please?" Judge Smiley said.

"Yes, Your Honor."

The three men were brought before the bench. Kelly Sims and Billy Purcell stood with their heads bowed contritely. Charley Harris smiled at the judge in arrogant defiance.

Judge Smiley cleared his throat. "You men have been tried before a jury of twelve men, honest and true, for the murders of Loren Hancock, Stephan Sinclair, Dr. Burl Presnell and his wife, Mary Presnell. You were ably represented by counsel—"

"You mean by an idiot," Charley interrupted.

"By court-appointed counsel," Judge Smiley went on. "And you have all been found guilty as charged."

"We know all that. Get on with it," Charley taunted.

The bailiff took a step toward Charley, but Judge Smiley nodded at him, and the bailiff stepped back.

"Additionally, you, Charley Harris—"

"Call me Cactus Charley, everyone else does," Charley interrupted. When the gallery laughed nervously, Charley turned toward them and held his arms over his head, with his handcuffed hands clasped. "These are my people, Judge," he said.

Judge Smiley banged his gavel several times for order, and when the gallery quieted, he glared at them.

"If there is one more demonstration, I will clear the court and hang these men in private," he growled.

The crowd, not wanting to miss the spectacle of the hanging, fell silent.

"And now, Mr. Harris," the judge continued. "As I was about to say, though you were only tried for those four deaths, you readily admit to the killing of others. Is this correct?"

"Yeah, so what?" Charley replied. "What are you going to do, hang me for each killin'?" He giggled.

"If that were possible, Mr. Harris, you may be assured that I would do so. Fortunately one hanging is all it will take. I normally ask God to have mercy upon the souls of those I condemn to the gallows, but for you, Mr. Harris, I offer no such prayer. Indeed, my only regret is that I cannot impose a sentence to be carried out in the hereafter."

"You go to hell, Judge," Charley spat.

"Exactly what I was talking about, Mr. Harris," Judge Smiley replied. "I am condemning your sorry soul to hell." He picked up his gavel and rapped it sharply against the pad on his desk.

"I sentence Kelly Sims, Billy Purcell, and most particularly you, Charles Harris, to join with your fellow murderer, Ray Barnett, where the four of you will be hanged by the neck until you are dead. Sentence will be carried out at two o'clock on this very afternoon."

There was a buzz of whispering excitement throughout the court as everyone realized that on this very day four prisoners would be hanged.

"Four! Four at one time, by God! This'll sure make a fitting end to all the stories those papers have been carryin' back East!" someone said excitedly.

"Silence! Silence in the court," Judge Smiley said, and again he slapped his gavel against the pad. The gallery grew quiet. "Deputy Carter, escort the condemned men to the holding cells. Court is dismissed."

"Who'll have tickets to the hanging?" the clerk called.

"Me! I want one!" someone called.

"Save one for me!"

The three prisoners, their legs hobbled with an eighteen-inch chain, were chained together for the move back to the cells. As the deputy escorted them out of the court and to the holding cell, they had to move with an awkward gait. They shuffled out as crowds of people pressed around the clerk to get the little blue ticket that would grant them access to the side courtyard where the hanging would take place.

The holding cell was separated from the main jail. It was out in the side courtyard, less than fifty feet from the gallows itself. There, the condemned prisoners would be able to look through the barred windows and watch the crowd gather and the excitement grow as time for their execution approached.

The deputy took them out through the side door of the courthouse, then across the sunbaked, dirt-packed courtyard toward the little holding cell. It was quiet in the yard since, as yet, no spectators had been allowed around the gallows.

They passed through the shadow of the gallows. Someone was up on the gallows deck, oiling the hinges to the trapdoor. He pulled the lever and the door swung open with a bang. Purcell let out a little cry of alarm. Charley laughed.

"Don't you fret none, Billy boy," Deputy Carter teased. "They're just greasin' the doors to hell for you." He laughed out loud at his own joke.

"You're gettin' a big kick out of this, ain't you, Dave?" Charley said.

The deputy smiled. "Watchin' you three boys hang is goin' to be like Christmas, New Year's, and my birthday all rolled into one," he said.

"Dave, I sure hope nothin' happens to upset your little plans," Charley said.

Carter laughed out loud. "Still makin' the jokes, I see. Well, you may as well enjoy what time you got left. I sure plan to."

"I'm glad I can be so entertainin'," Charley said. He pointed toward the outhouse. "Hey Dave, before you put us in our cells, how about lettin' me take a leak?"

"You just wait awhile," Carter answered.

"Accordin' to what the judge just said, I don't have all that long to wait for anything," Charley replied. "Besides, you want me to pee in my pants? Now, that would be a pretty sight for the ladies that come to see the hangin', won't it?"

Carter looked around the courtyard. Except for the worker on the gallows, and Ray Barnett, whose face was behind bars in his cell, no one else was in sight.

"All right," he finally relented. "I'll let you take a leak. But be quick about it."

"Thanks," Charley said. "You are goin' to cut me loose from the others, aren't you? I don't care to have them all goin' in there with me."

Carter laughed. "Why, Charley, I never knew you were such a shy man," he said. He bent down to unlock the chain. He didn't notice that the man who had been working on the gallows had come down and was walking over toward him. As soon as he was even with the deputy, he pulled a gun and pointed it at Carter's head.

"Unlock the hobble chain, too," the gallows worker said. "And get the others."

Carter looked up in surprise, then his face reflected his shock. "Why, you ain't Homer," he gasped. "Where's Homer? Who are you?"

"I'm the man that's already killed Homer and I'm gonna blow your brains out too, if you don't do what I tell you to," the man with the gun answered. He smiled, showing stained, crooked teeth. His eyes were yellow and one of them was half-covered with a drooping eyelid. A puffed, ugly scar started on the forehead just above that drooping eye, passed through the lid then under the eye, and hooked around the bottom of his nose. "Now unlock those hobbles like I said."

"Good man, Lucas," Charley said, giggling happily. He looked at the others. "Well, boys, you didn't really think I was just goin' to let us all die, did you? This here is Lucas Babbit, the only man ever to beat Sam Slater."

"I'm real pleased to meet you, Lucas!" Purcell said happily.

"Me, too," Sims added.

"Charley! Charley, don't forget me!" Barnett called from the cell.

"Sorry, Ray. You're still ailin' some from your wound. You ain't quite up to hard ridin' yet," Charley called back.

"You can't leave me here to hang!"

Charley giggled. "Why not? All these people are comin' to town for the show. We got to give them somethin', ain't we?"

From behind the courthouse a rider appeared, leading four horses.

"You gents hurry up," the rider urged. "I had to knife the guard at the back gate."

Suddenly two guards came into the courtyard from the front of the building.

"Stop!" one of them shouted. He fired a shot, which missed. Charley, armed now, returned fire and he didn't miss. The guard who had fired collapsed with a hole in his chest. The other guard, suddenly realizing that he was alone, retreated around the corner.

"We've got to get out of here!" Purcell shouted.

"Wait a minute," Charley said. "I got a little business to take care of first." He looked at the deputy and started smiling.

The deputy, realizing what was on Charley's

mind, began to tremble in fear, and he held his hands out in front of him.

"Now, Charley, you don't want to shoot me," he said. "What good will that do you?"

"Oh, it'll do me a world of good, Dave. More good than you'll ever know," Charley said with a broad, evil smile. He raised his gun and fired. A bullet hole appeared in the deputy's forehead, then he pitched back.

"Come on, boys, let's ride!" Charley shouted, swinging into his saddle.

"Don't leave me, you bastards! Don't leave me here like this!" Barnett shouted in vain.

By now the shouts and gunfire had alerted the others, and several armed men appeared in the courtyard, just in time to see the five riders gallop through the back gate. They fired at the outlaws but not one bullet found its mark. Lucas Babbit, Charley Harris, and the entire band had gotten away.

That same afternoon

NEARLY THREE HUNDRED PEOPLE WERE gathered in the courtyard to watch Ray Barnett hang. Many, who had not yet heard of the mass escape, thought they were coming to see four men hanged. When they learned otherwise, they were openly vocal in their disappointment at being cheated out of such a grand spectacle. But, they told each other, it wasn't a total loss after all. At least one of the outlaws would hang this afternoon.

Enterprising vendors made the best of the

situation, passing through the crowd selling lemonade, beer, pretzels, popcorn, and sweet rolls. In one corner of the courtyard a black-frocked preacher stood on an overturned box, delivering a sermon full of fire and brimstone and warnings of perdition.

On the second floor of the courtroom, Judge Smiley stood at the window of his chambers and looked down on the proceedings. Sam Slater was just behind him, lighting a cigar that he had extracted from a humidor on the judge's desk.

"I told you I'd pay the money and I will," Judge Smiley said to the man standing behind him looking out the window. "There's fifteen hundred dollars in that brown envelope on my desk."

Sam reached for it.

"The territory will pay another fifteen hundred to get them back, and I'll see to it that the court adds fifteen hundred more. That's three thousand dollars more," Judge Smiley offered.

"Three thousand dollars?" Sam said, stroking the scar on the side of his face. "You know, Judge, with that kind of reward money out there, you're just going to make it harder to find them. There will be too many people trying to get the reward and they'll be getting in the way."

Judge Smiley turned away from the window. "That reward isn't for everyone," he said. "I'm only offering that to you."

"You're not putting out new dodgers?"

Judge Smiley shook his head. "No," he said.

"That kind of money is pretty persuasive," Sam replied.

"That's what I'm countin' on. I particularly want these men, Slater," the judge said. He pulled the curtain aside to watch as the hangman checked the single rope that hung from the beam, the noose at its end yawning in grotesque emptiness.

"What about the two fellas who helped them escape? Anything on them?"

"Not more than ten minutes ago Barnett give us the name of one of them," Judge Smiley replied. "Said he'd tell us the other name if we'd commute his sentence. Of course, I told him we wouldn't make any deals."

"What name did he give you?"

"Babbit. Lucas Babbit."

"Lucas Babbit?" Sam said, looking up in interest.

Judge Smiley chuckled. "I thought you might be interested," he said.

"Yeah, I'm interested."

"Now, mind you, I can't add anything for him, or for the other fella, whoever he was. It's taking all I've got just to up the ante on Harris and his boys."

"You don't need to add anything for Babbit," Sam said. "Even if there was no reward for him, I'd bring that sorry son of a bitch in for free."

"The reward is for dead or alive," Judge Smiley said. "But if you can, I want them alive. I want to hang these men."

"I make no promises," Sam said.

"You'll at least try to get them here alive?"

"I make no promises," Sam said again.

Judge Smiley stroked his chin for a long moment before he answered. "All right," he said. "I've sentenced them to die. I guess the manner of their execution doesn't really matter. You do whatever it takes."

Ray Barnett looked around defiantly as he was led to the gallows. He was wearing a gray, collarless shirt and gray trousers. His legs weren't hobbled, but his hands were handcuffed behind his back. He squirted out a stream of tobacco juice just as he reached the foot of the thirteen steps, then he hesitated.

"Get on up there, Barnett," Sheriff McQuade said. "You done your killin' like a man, now die like one."

Barnett turned around to glare at him. "Sheriff, you don't have to give me no lessons on how to die," he said.

"Come on, Ray," McQuade said more gently. "The sooner we get this over with, the better it is for all of us."

Barnett moved onto the scaffold, then was

positioned under the noose. From here he had a very good look into the faces of the spectators, and he glared at them defiantly.

The clergyman who had been preaching hell and damnation now walked up to the condemned man. "Mr. Barnett, do you want to repent?" he asked.

"What have I got to repent for?"

"Why, you have killed, sir."

Barnett looked out over the faces of the crowd. "Yeah? Well, what do you think you people are about to do?"

"The authorities are merely executing their God-given right," the preacher said.

"And the folks here? Is it their God-given right to enjoy watchin' me dance?"

"I beg of you, sir. Repent. Repent now, before it is too late."

"I ain't repentin' for a goddamned thing."

"Mr. Barnett!" the preacher said angrily. "You are goin' to meet God with heresy in your heart and blasphemy on your lips! You'll spend an eternity in hell for that!"

"Thanks for the words, preacher," Barnett said sarcastically. "They're real comfortin'."

The preacher, red-faced with anger, turned and walked quickly off the scaffold.

"Any last words, Barnett?" Sheriff McQuade asked. McQuade was having to serve as the hangman, since Lucas Babbit had killed the man who was supposed to do the job.

"Yeah. I wonder what they'll be servin' for supper in hell?" Barnett asked. "Whatever it is, it's bound to be better'n that pig swill you serve in this jail."

"I don't know, but when you get there, say hello to a few of my friends for me, will you?" McQuade asked.

"McQuade, you want me to hold you a place at the supper table?" Barnett asked as the black hood was slipped over his head.

McQuade chuckled. "That's nice of you, Ray. Real nice," he said. "It's time." He fit the noose. "When the trap opens, don't hunch up your shoulders," he added, trying to be helpful. "Just relax and it'll be better."

"Really? How the hell do you know?" Barnett mumbled from under his hood.

When McQuade had him ready, he stepped over to the handle that would open the trapdoor. He glanced up toward the window where Judge Smiley stood looking down. Smiley nodded his head and the hangman pulled the handle.

The trapdoor swung down on its hinges and Barnett's body dropped about five feet. There was an almost orgasmic gasp from the crowd as the body fell.

Barnett didn't die right away. For almost four minutes after he fell through the trapdoor he kept drawing his body up as if in that way he could relieve the weight on his neck. His stomach heaved, and those nearest the scaffold could hear rasping sounds from his throat. Finally his body was still.

"Ghastly business, this," Judge Smiley said, pouring himself a drink with shaking hands. He looked over at Sam. "You're a fellow who lives your life right on the edge, aren't you, Mr. Slater?"

"You might say that," Sam agreed.

Judge Smiley tossed his drink down. "Watch your step," he said. "I wouldn't want ever to see you up there on my gallows."

"Don't worry, Judge," Sam replied matter-of-factly. "If it ever came to that . . . you wouldn't live long enough to see it."

Nervously Judge Smiley poured himself yet another drink.

The sound of a shot rolled down the mountainside, picked up resonance, then echoed back from the neighboring mountains. Charley Harris, who was holding a smoking pistol, turned toward his audience of four with a smile on his face. He had just shattered a tossed whiskey bottle with his marksmanship.

"I'd like to see Slater do that," he snarled.

"Charley, there ain't nobody said you ain't good with a gun," Purcell said. "Maybe even as good as Slater, but—"

"*Maybe* as good? Maybe as good?"

"Well, as good then. Maybe even better—"

"There ain't no maybe to it. I *am* better."

"But even if you are, that don't matter. You seen how that sneaky bastard come up on us the last time. He got the drop on us afore we even had a notion he was anywhere around. I say we don't take no chances this time."

"And what do you propose that we do?" Charley asked.

"I think we ought to split up . . . ever' man for hisself. The son of a bitch can't follow us all at the same time."

"No, but he can follow just one of us," Sims pointed out. "And woe betide the one that he follows."

"Yeah? Well, I ain' afraid of the son of a bitch," Lucas Babbit said.

"You mean you don't care if he gets on your tail?" Purcell asked.

"Hell, he's been on my tail for more'n a year," Babbit replied. "What I ought to do is quit runnin'. I ought to just wait behind a rock and shoot him down."

"You mean you'd shoot him from ambush?" Charley asked.

"Hell, yes. I ain't like you, Charley. I ain't tryin' to build myself no reputation. I don't need to kill the son of a bitch fair and square . . . I just want to kill him."

"Lucas has a point," Sims said. "The best

way to handle someone like Slater would be to set up an ambush."

"All right, even if that's true, don't you think it would be better for us all to stick together?"

"No," Sims replied. "I still think it would be best if he didn't even find us at all, and if we split up, we'll have a better chance."

"Except for the one he comes after," Purcell pointed out.

"All right," Charley said. "How about this? Instead of all of us separatin', we'll break into two groups, one of three and one of two. That way he'll still have to make a choice, but even when he does, we'll have him outnumbered."

"All right, I'll go along with that," Sims said.

"This is the way we'll do it," Charley explained. "Kelly, you and Jeb Scruggs cut out one way, me an' Billy and Lucas will go another. Now, whichever ones of us gets wind that he ain't on our trail, why, we'll double back and help out. That way we'll have him pinched right in the middle."

"Why that's a wonderful idea!" Purcell said, smiling broadly. He chuckled. "Charley, you shoulda been a general."

IT WAS FOUR DAYS BEFORE SAM CAME across a fresh trail. The men he was after had split up, two going in one direction, three going in the other. Kelly Sims and another man—the bartender wasn't sure who the other man was—had stopped in the town of Posey for a drink, and by the time they were on their way again, Sam had nearly caught up with them.

Sims took great pains to cover his true trail while leaving false trails for Sam to follow. Sims and whoever it was with him rode through streams and over hard rock, trying every trick in the book to shake off their pursuer, but doggedly, Sam hung on.

Once, while following them through a draw in Red Rock Mesa, Sims and his partner started a rock slide. It was a desperate move on their part and they really didn't intend to do much more than slow him down a bit, but the rock slide nearly caught him, and Sam had to turn his horse and gallop hard to get out of the way.

"Damn!" Scruggs said. "We almost got the son of a bitch!"

"Yeah, well, almost ain't good enough," Sims said. "The bastard is still alive, and he's still after us."

"What are we goin' to do, Kelly? You got 'ny ideas?"

"No," Sims answered.

"What if we just wait behind some rocks somewhere and ambush him, like Lucas said?"

Sims shook his head. "If we don't get him right off, he'll get behind a rock hisself, then we'll be in a gunfight with him. I don't know about you, Jeb, but I don't cotton to bein' in no gunfight with Sam Slater . . . not with just the two of us."

"Well it ain't supposed to be just the two of us," Scruggs reminded him. "Charley said him and the others would come a-runnin' if they seen that Slater wasn't after them."

"Yeah? Well, where the hell are they?" Sims asked. "Do you see any sign of 'em?"

"No," Scruggs admitted.

"No, an' you ain't likely to," Sims told him.

Twenty miles south

"Did you see anything back there, Billy?" Charley asked when Purcell scrambled back down from the promontory, his boots dislodging pebbles and small rocks.

"No, nothin'," Purcell replied. He brushed his hands together. "I looked as far as I could in all directions, and I didn't see even a piece of a dust plume. I don't think he's followin' us."

Charley took a drink of water, wiped the back of his hand across his mouth, then corked his canteen and hooked it back on the saddle pommel.

"Well, then he must've lit out after Kelly and Jeb."

"We goin' to double back?" Purcell asked.

"Double back? What for?"

"You said we was goin' to double back if we seen that Slater wasn't doggin' us."

"Yeah, well, Kelly is the one who wanted us all to separate," Charley said. "We done what he wanted, so far's I'm concerned now, Kelly and Jeb is on their own. Unless you want to go back and tangle with Slater on your own."

"You think I'm crazy? If you two ain't goin' back, I sure as hell ain't."

"I didn't figure you was that dumb," Charley said. "Anyway, the way I look at it, Slater takin' out after them like he done just makes it all the better for us."

"Yeah," Purcell said. He smiled. "Yeah, I guess you're right at that. While Kelly an' Jeb is keeping' Slater busy we'll be runnin'."

Charley chuckled. "Oh, we'll be doin' more than runnin'," he said.

"More than runnin'? What do you mean?"

"You mighta noticed that we ain't got two coppers to rub together. Don't you think it would be good to have a little money to do our runnin' on?"

"Yeah, it would be," Purcell replied. "You got 'ny ideas?"

"Lucas seen a bank over in Salcedo the other day."

"Salcedo? I don't know the town."

"It's a little flyspeck of a town," Babbit offered. "They ain't got no law 'cept for a sheriff who's so old he can barely get around. That bank's just beggin' to be robbed."

"How much you reckon could be in a bank like that?" Purcell asked.

"Prob'ly not too much. A thousand dollars, tops," Babbit admitted. "But that's the beauty of it, don't you see? If there ain't a whole lot of money in the bank, then they're not goin' to be expectin' anyone to rob it. Hell, they'll prob'ly pee in their pants when we go in. It'll be like takin' candy from a baby."

"Yeah, but if it's not too much money, is it worth it?"

"Well, now, that all depends," Charley said. "How much money you got now?"

Purcell smiled. "Yeah," he said. "Yeah, I see what you are talkin' about."

Twenty miles north

"He's still comin'," Scruggs said.

Sims twisted around in his saddle. "How far back is he? Did you see him?"

"Yeah, I got a glimpse of 'im just over the last ridge."

"That'd make him less'n a mile back."

"Ain't they no way we can shake him?" Scruggs asked.

"You got 'ny ideas that we ain't tried?" Sims replied. "We done ever'thing I can think of, an' it ain't even slowed 'im down none."

"So what do you want to do now? You want to wait behind a couple of rocks and shoot him, like I suggested?"

"No. I told you, I don't want to get into a gunfight with him unless the odds are a little better."

"Pretty soon we ain't goin' to have no choice," Scuggs pointed out. "He's back there, he's comin', and they ain't nothin' on earth goin' to stop him from catchin' us. Then we're goin' to have to shoot it out with him sure enough, only by then he'll be choosing the time and the place."

"Yeah, well, there is one thing we could do," Sims suggested, "if you're game for it."

"Hell, I'm willin' to try 'bout anythin'," Scruggs said. "What you got in mind?"

"We could split up again. You go one way and I'll go the other."

"Well, now, hold it. That don't make no sense to me at all. I mean here you are bitchin' because you say two to one ain't the right kind of odds to go up against him. But you're wantin' us to split up so it'll be one to one."

"It'll be one to one for whoever's trail he dogs," Sims said. "But the other one of us can get away free and clear. That'll give each one of us a fifty-fifty chance of not havin' to run into him at all. And for whichever one of us that does run into him, well, hell, we won't be no worse off than we are now."

"Yeah, all right," Scruggs said, stroking his chin. "I guess them odds is about as good as any. Which way you aimin' to go?"

"I thought I might go west," Sims said.

"All right, you go west, I'll go south," Scruggs replied. He smiled crookedly at Sims. "I ain't goin' to wish you luck," he said. "'Cause if your luck is runnin' good, that'll mean mine is runnin' bad."

"Yeah," Sims said. "I know what you mean. Maybe we'll see each other around sometime."

"Maybe," Scruggs replied. He slapped his heels against his horse's flanks, then started down the middle of a small stream, heading south.

Sims started west, but after a few moments he reined up and looked back to the point where he and Scruggs had separated. Scruggs was out of sight now, and because he had gone down the middle of the stream, there was absolutely no sign that he had been there at all.

Sims saw a willow tree, its boughs hanging low over the water, and he suddenly got an idea. He rode back into the stream, up to the tree, then he reached up and broke off two of the branches. After that he rode back into the rocks, got off his horse and tied it down. He pulled the Winchester from its saddle sheath and bellied down between two rocks, where he not only had cover and concealment, but a good view of the willow tree as well. He jacked a round into the chamber, then piled a couple of rocks on top of each other to make a rest for the rifle. He sighted down the barrel, then waited.

When Sam reached the edge of the stream, he stopped. If the two men he was after followed the pattern, they would use the stream for as long as they could to avoid leaving a trail. For most trackers, that ploy would work. Slater, however, could often follow a trail through the water by paying attention to such things as rocks dislodged against the flow of water, or silt, which when disturbed by a horse's hooves would leave a little pattern in the water for several minutes.

Sam was about to check the stream bed when he saw something unusual. There were two limbs broken in the willow tree that hung over the bank of the stream.

That was strange, he thought. In the first place, the limbs should have been supple enough not to be broken by someone passing through them. And in the second place, it would be foolish for someone on the dodge to ride through the limbs anyway. They were close enough to the edge of the stream that they could easily avoid them. It was almost as if they had been broken on purpose.

Sam realized that they *had* been broken on purpose, and in almost the same instant the hair pricked on the back of his neck. Someone had the drop on him. Suddenly, and unexpectedly, Sam threw himself off his horse. At almost the precise instant he made his move, a rifle boomed and a .44-40 bullet cracked through the air at exactly the place where his head had been but a second earlier.

Sam hit the water feetfirst and ran through the stream, splashing silver sheets of spray as he headed for the opposite side. He zigzaged as he ran, and when the rifle boomed a second time, the strike of the bullet in the water demonstrated the wisdom of his erratic motion, for it hit where he would have been had he run in a straight line.

Sam dived into the tall grass on the bank of the stream, then wriggled on his belly toward the protection of a large rock, about ten yards away. Though he was concealed by the grass, he wasn't protected by it, and a lucky shot would be disastrous.

Sam bent over a large cattail and hooked his hat on top. He found a fairly long branch and used it to hold the cattail down while he backed away from it, moving himself closer to the protection offered by the boulder. When he was as far away from the cattail as the long branch would let him be, he let go and the cattail, with his hat on top, sprang back up to the upright position.

Almost instantly the rifle boomed again and Sam saw his hat go flying. He used that opportunity to move the last few feet to the boulder. There, he sat with his back against the rock and took a few deep breaths.

"Slater? Slater, are you hit?"

Sam recognized Kelly Sims's voice.

"You weren't even close, Sims," Sam called from behind the rock.

Sam heard Sims gasp in surprise, for not

only was Sam not where Sims expected him to be, he had also not been hit.

"You son of a bitch!" Sims shouted. He fired two more times in the vicinity of where he had heard Sam's voice, but the bullets whistled by, harmlessly, overhead.

"Why don't you give up, Sims?" Sam called.

"Give up? And go back to be hung?"

Sam chuckled. "I'll admit you don't have much to look forward to," he said. "But you may as well know I'm taking you out of here, in your saddle or belly-down on it. Now, which is it to be?"

"Let me think about it a moment."

"Don't take too long," Sam said.

There was a long moment of silence, then Sims called again. "Slater, you ever thought you might've followed the same trail I rode? 'Could be you was the one with a price on your head and not me."

"Could've been," Sam admitted, without confessing that he did have a price on his head.

"I mean, when you stop and think about it, we ain't all that different, are we?"

"I don't shoot innocent women," Sam replied.

"If you talkin' about the doc's wife, it was Charley that shot her."

"You didn't make effort to stop him."

"No, I reckon I didn't," Sims replied.

Suddenly, and unexpectedly, Sam heard the

sound of a horse's hooves, and when he raised up and looked around, he saw that Sims had managed to get mounted and was now galloping toward him. Sims had his pistol in his hand and he was firing at Sam as he rode. One bullet clipped through Sam's collar, coming close enough to take a small nick out of his neck.

When Sam fired back, he saw a puff of dust rising from Sims's vest, followed by a tiny spray of blood. Sims pitched backward out of his saddle. One foot hung up in the stirrup and his horse continued to run, raising a plume of water as Sims was dragged through the stream. As the horse tried to climb the bank out of the water, Sims' foot disconnected from the stirrup and he lay, motionless, half in the water and half out.

Sam ran over to him, his gun still drawn. When he saw that Sims was unarmed, having lost his pistol during the dragging across the stream, he holstered his gun and pulled the outlaw out of the water. He was surprised to see that Sims was still breathing, though the rattle of his breathing told Sam that he wouldn't be alive much longer.

"That was a damn fool thing to do," Sam said.

Sims tried to laugh, but when he did so, bubbles of blood frothed out from the corner of his mouth.

"I reckon it was," he admitted. "But there

wasn't no way I was goin' to let you take me back to be hung. To tell the truth, I was hopin' you'd shoot me."

"Where are the others?" Sam asked.

Sims, who had closed his eyes in pain, now opened them and looked at Sam. "You think I'm goin' to tell you that?"

"You don't owe any of them anything," Sam advised him.

"Hell, Slater, I know that," Sims replied. "That ain't the reason I ain't goin' to tell you nothin'. I ain't tellin' you nothin' 'cause it's the only way I got now of gettin' at you."

"It makes no difference whether you tell me or not," Sam said. "I'll find them."

Again, Sims tried to laugh, and again bubbles of blood frothed from his mouth.

"Yeah, you prob'ly will. But if it takes you just one day longer, then I figure I'll have my laugh." Sims suddenly took two or three gasping breaths, then he died.

FROM TWO MILES AWAY SAM COULD SEE THE little town of Risco baking under the sun. It was hot, dry, dusty, and as brittle as a tumbleweed. He had filled his and Sims's canteen at the stream and kept both canteens for himself, figuring Sims, who was belly-down on the horse behind him, wouldn't mind.

Even with two canteens Sam had practiced water rationing, but here, with civilization of sorts right in front of him, he allowed himself to drink the final few swallows of one of the canteens. The water was warm, but his tongue was swollen and dry, so that any moisture, regardless of temperature, was welcome. And although he was drinking tepid water, he could almost taste the cool beer he would have in the saloon in town.

Sam hooked his canteen back onto the saddle pommel then urged the two horses, the one he was riding and the one he was leading, forward. The buildings in the town had collected the day's heat and were now giving it back in waves, so that Risco seemed to shimmer in the distance. A dust devil developed in front of him, propelled by a wind that felt as if it were blowing straight from the fires of hell. A jackrabbit popped up, ran for several feet, then darted under a dusty clump of mesquite.

It took the better part of a quarter of an hour to reach the town, and he rode in slowly, sizing it up with wary eyes. It was a town with only one street. The unpainted wood of the few ramshackle buildings was turning gray and splitting. There was no railroad coming into Risco, but there was a stagecoach station with a schedule board announcing the arrival and departure of four stagecoaches per week. He had known many towns like this—isolated, desolate, and stagnant.

Sam rode past the buildings, subconsciously enumerating them as he passed. There was a rooming house, a livery, a smithy's, and a general store that said DRUGS, MEATS, GOODS on its high, false front. There was a hotel and restaurant, too, and, of course, the obligatory saloon . . . this one called the Red Star. Across the street from the saloon was the jail. Sam rode up to the hitching rail in front of the jail, dismounted, and patted his shirt and pants a few times. The action sent up puffs of white dust, which hovered around him like a cloud. Sam looked up and down the street. A few buildings away a door slammed while, across the street, an isinglass shade came down on the upstairs window of the hotel. A sign creaked in the wind and flies buzzed loudly around the piles of horse manure that lay in the street.

Sam pushed open the door. No one was at the desk, but someone was sleeping in one of the bunks in a cell. The door to that cell, like the door to all the others, was standing open. Except for this one, all the cells were empty.

Sam walked over to the wall where several posters were tacked and began studying them. He had left the door to the building standing open, and a gust of wind blew it shut with a loud bang.

"What? What?" the man in the cell said, awakened by the loud pop. He sat up on the bunk and saw Sam standing by his poster wall. "Who are you?" he asked.

Sam looked toward him. "You a prisoner?" he asked.

"A prisoner? Hell no, I'm not a prisoner," the man said indignantly. "I'm the sheriff, by God!"

"I got a body for you," Sam said.

"A body? Where?"

"Belly-down across his horse," Sam said. "He's tied up out front."

"Who is it?"

Sam saw a poster with Kelly Sims's name and picture, and he tore it down. "This man," he said.

The sheriff, who was bald-headed and overweight, came out of the cell poking his shirt down into his trousers. "The hell you say. Kelly Sims, huh? He's a bad one. Did you kill him?"

"Yes."

"I suppose you'll be puttin' in for the reward?"

Sam glared at the sheriff. "I didn't kill him for the sport of it," he said.

"No, I don't reckon you did. Well, let me take a look at him and I'll send a wire back," the sheriff said, starting toward the door. "Who will I say is puttin' in for the reward?"

The sheriff stopped in his tracks and looked back toward Sam. "You . . . you the one they call the Regulator?"

"Sometimes," Sam said. He held out the posters on Charley Harris, Billy Purcell, and Lucas Babbit. "Any of these men been through here?" he asked.

"I don't know," the sheriff said. "And the truth is, if they had, I would've given 'em a wide berth. The only job I got is to keep the peace in Risco. I ain't in the manhuntin' business. Once I get confirmation on Sims's body, where will I find you?"

"I'll be in the saloon across the street," Sam said.

Inside the saloon, Jeb Scruggs was eating biscuits and gravy at a table in the back when he saw Sam Slater push his way through the bat-wing doors. Though this was the first time Jeb had seen him up close, there was no doubt in his mind as to who it was. With the purple scar and hard eyes, the stranger fit, perfectly, the description Kelly Sims had given him.

For a moment Scruggs panicked, and it was all he could do to keep from getting up and bolting through the back door. His hands began to shake so badly that he couldn't hold his fork and he had to put them down on the table in front of him.

"Beer," he heard Slater say to the bartender.

The bartender drew a beer and handed it to Slater. The bounty hunter blew off the head then drank nearly three quarters of it before he put it down. Then he wiped his mouth with the back of his hand and turned his back to the bar to look out over the patrons.

Damn! He's looking right at me! Scruggs thought. He grew tense, waiting for Slater to pull his gun, waiting for the bullet to come slamming into his chest.

But nothing happened.

Slater looked right toward Scruggs, then passed his eyes around the rest of the room, showing no recognition whatever.

Scruggs smiled broadly. The son of a bitch didn't recognize me! he thought. He's been chasing me all this time and he doesn't even know who I am!

Sam finished the beer, then turned toward the barkeep to ask for another when suddenly something flashed by in front of him. It was a knife! The blade buried itself about half an inch into the bar with a thocking sound. After that, the handle vibrated back and forth.

Instantly Sam drew his pistol and turned toward the direction from which the knife had come. He saw a man getting up from a table with a gun in his hand. However, when that man saw how quickly Sam had drawn, he held his hands up, letting the pistol dangle from its trigger guard.

"No, no," he said. "Don't shoot, mister. Don't shoot!"

"Why the hell not?" Sam growled. "If you

would've had your way, I'd be wearing that Arkansas toothpick by now."

"My God, mister, you're not real, you know that? How did you find me? I didn't leave any more of a trail than a bird would. What does a man have to do to get rid of you?"

Sam chuckled. "The truth is, mister, I lost your trail back there in the stream. The only reason I came into town was to turn Sims over to the sheriff."

"You got Sims in jail?"

Sam shook his head. "By now I reckon the sheriff has him down to the undertaker," he said.

"You mean . . . you didn't follow me here, to Risco?"

Sam shook his head again. "I didn't even know you were the one I was after until you tried to stick me with that Arkansas toothpick."

"Maybe not," Scruggs replied. "But you woulda found me soon enough. The way I figured it, I didn't have no choice."

"You didn't figure it very well. Where are the others?" Sam asked. "Harris, Purcell, Babbit?"

"You think I'm going to tell you that?"

"Why not? As long as you're talking, I'm not shooting," Sam reminded him.

The outlaw smiled, then, slowly, turned the pistol around so that the butt was pointing toward Sam.

"You ain't goin' to shoot anyway," he said. "I've done give up, and this here saloon is full of witnesses who'll swear I was handin' you my gun. You shoot me now, you'll hang."

"Who the hell are you?" Sam asked.

"You mean to tell me you don't even know my name?"

"I never heard anyone say," Sam replied. "All I know is you're one of the two men who helped Harris and his bunch escape," Sam said. "Barnett identified Babbit as one of the men, but he didn't tell us your name."

"The name is Scruggs, Jeb Scruggs. You heard of me?"

"Yeah, I've heard of you."

Scruggs smiled. "I must be doin' pretty good for the Regulator to have heard of me."

Until now, everyone in the bar had been looking on in fascinated silence. They had realized that Sam was some sort of lawman who had just found his quarry. But until Scruggs said the name, they had no idea they were in the presence of the famous bounty hunter.

"The Regulator?" someone in the bar said. "Did you hear what he called the man? This here is the Regulator." That was followed by a buzz of excitement as everyone strained to get a close look at the man who had earned such a reputation.

"All right, Scruggs," Sam said. "I'm going to park you across the street in this jail until I find the others. If you're real nice to the sheriff, he might feed you."

"You ain't scarin' me none, Slater. This here seems like a nice enough town to me. I don't mind coolin' my heels here for a while. You goin' to take my gun or ain't you?"

Sam started across the floor for Scruggs's gun, but before he went half a step, Scruggs executed as neat a border roll as Sam had ever seen. He wasn't often caught by surprise, but this time he was . . . not only by the fact that Scruggs would try such a thing, but by the skill with which the man was able to do it.

Sam had relaxed his own position to the point where he had actually let the hammer down on his pistol and even lowered the gun. Now he had to raise the gun back into line while at the same time cocking it. And he was at a disadvantage given that Scruggs had acted first.

The quiet room was suddenly shattered with the roar of two pistols snapping firing caps and exploding powder almost simultaneously. The bar patrons yelled and dived or scrambled for cover. White gun smoke billowed out in a cloud that filled the center of the room, momentarily obscuring everything.

As the smoke began to clear, Scruggs stared through the white cloud, smiling broadly at Sam. He opened his mouth as if to speak. The only sound he made, however, was a gagging rattle, way back in his throat. The smile left his face, his eyes glazed over, and he pitched forward, his gun clattering to the floor.

Sam stood ready to fire a second shot if needed, but a second shot wasn't necessary. He looked down at Scruggs for a moment, then holstered his pistol.

There were calls from outside, then the sound of people running. Several came into the saloon and stood under the rising cloud of gun smoke to stare in wonderment at the dead man on the floor. One of the new arrivals was the sheriff.

"Mister, death seems to follow you like a black cloud," the sheriff observed. He pointed at the body on the floor. "This your doin'?"

"Yes," Sam answered. "I had no choice, you can ask anyone."

"That's right, Sheriff, this here fella shot first," someone said.

The sheriff nodded. "He one of the ones you're after?"

Sam nodded. "He helped Charley Harris and the others escape," he said. "In the escape they killed two guards, the hangman, and a deputy sheriff."

"Yeah, I heard about that, even down here," the sheriff said. "Who is this fella?"

"His name is Scruggs. Jeb Scruggs."

"Don't recognize the name. Is there paper on him, too?"

"Yeah," Sam said.

The sheriff sighed. "I just sent the wire about Kelly Sims," he said. "I reckon I can send another one."

"I'm obliged."

"What about the body?" the sheriff asked.

Sam shrugged. "That's your department now, Sheriff. Dead or alive, I turn him over to you. Put him alongside Kelly Sims. They're birds of a feather." As Sam talked to the sheriff he knelt beside Scruggs's body and began going through the outlaw's pockets.

"I thought you said the body was mine," the sheriff said.

"The body is yours," Sam replied. "What I find in his pockets is mine. Anyway, you haven't signed the receipt yet."

Sam found a money clip containing twenty dollars in paper currency. In addition to the bills, there were fifteen dollars in coin. He handed the coin to the sheriff. "You can use this to bury him," he said.

"Thanks," the sheriff replied, putting the coins in his pocket.

Sam had not gone through Scruggs's pockets for the money, but to see if he could get any clue as to where the others might be. Other than the money, however, he found nothing.

After Scruggs's body was dragged out of the saloon and the excitement caused by the event died down, Sam sat at the same table where Scruggs had been sitting and ordered a meal of bacon, eggs, and coffee. Back in the kitchen he saw a boy sweeping the floor and he motioned to him. When the boy came out to the table, Sam gave him a coin and asked him to take care of his horse. His supper had just been put before him when the boy returned.

"I put up your horse, mister," the boy said.

"Thanks."

"Was he a bad man? The one you killed?"

"Yes," Sam replied.

The boy smiled. "I thought he was. I could tell."

"How could you tell?"

"His eyes," the boy said, moving his fingers across his own eyes. "They were evil. His smile was not happy. He drank a lot and he kept watching the door. I believe he was looking for you."

"I reckon he was looking for me," Sam agreed. "You have a good eye."

The boy smiled proudly. "Someday, soon, I am going to leave Risco and become a bounty hunter, just like you," he said.

"Your mother and dad may want you to wait until you are a little older."

"I have no parents," the boy said.

"Where do you live?"

"Mr. Kingsley lets me stay in a nice room in

the stable and charges me nothing because I muck out the stalls for him. Mr. Beeson, who owns this saloon, gives me three meals a day because I sweep the floors for him. I have a good life."

Sam thought of his own orphaned boyhood and how he had been little more than a slave to his uncle. It would have been much better had he been on his own, like this boy. Others might feel sorry for the boy, but Sam knew that he was serious when he said he had a good life. Sam smiled. "I guess you do at that," he said.

SAM HAD TAKEN A ROOM IN THE FRONT OF the hotel, and the next morning a series of loud popping noises woke him from the soundest sleep he had enjoyed in days. Startled, he sat straight up in bed, slipped his pistol from the holster that hung from the bedpost, then got to his feet, ready for any intrusion.

There was another series of loud pops, followed by the high peal of a woman's laughter, then the sound of a brass band.

Sam moved over to the window and pulled the curtain to one side as he looked down on the street. The street was full of men and women, all dressed in their most colorful finery. There seemed to be a parade of some sort in progress, led by the brass band and a troupe of acrobatic dancers, followed by a highly polished brass, fire-engine pumper. The smell of food cooking over open fires filled the soft, morning air, and Sam decided he would go down to have breakfast and to see what was going on.

Fifteen minutes later he was eating a bacon-and-biscuit sandwich as he watched the celebration. When the sheriff saw Sam, he smiled and came over to him.

"I haven't been keeping up with the date," Sam said. "Is it the Fourth of July?"

The sheriff laughed. "The Fourth of July? No, that was two months ago."

"Really? Then what's the celebration?"

"Why, you're the cause of our celebration," the sheriff replied. "You mean you haven't figured that out yet?"

"What the hell are you talking about? How am I the cause of your celebration?"

"I take it you haven't gone down to look at the display on the porch of the general store," the sheriff asked.

"No."

"Go take a look, Mr. Slater. I think you'll be proud."

Finishing his biscuit, Sam walked down toward the general store. There were several people—men, women, and children—standing around the front porch looking at whatever it was the sheriff said was displayed there. When Sam got closer, he drew in a sharp breath of surprise.

There, in a pair of wooden coffins standing up against the wall, were the bodies of Kelly Sims and Jeb Scruggs. Both outlaws were dressed in black suits and their arms were crossed across their chest. Sims held a pistol in his right hand and nothing in his left. Scruggs clutched a pistol in his left hand while in his right he held the knife he had thrown at Sam. Sims's eyes were closed, but Scruggs's were open, though the left eyelid was half-closed. Scruggs's mouth was closed, but Sims's was open in what appeared to be a snarl. Sam had killed both men with bullets to the heart. Because of that, their wounds weren't visible.

"It's the Regulator!" someone shouted, noticing Sam looking at the bodies.

"The Regulator!"

"Three cheers for the Regulator!" someone else called. "Hip, hip . . ."

"Hooray!"

"Hip, hip . . ."

"Hooray!"

"Hip, hip . . ."

"Hooray!"

Sam held up his hand to silence them, then walked up for a closer look at a hand-lettered sign propped up at the foot of the coffins:

> HERE ARE THE BODIES OF THE BANDITS
> KELLY SIMS AND JEB SCRUGGS, KILLED
> BY THE REGULATOR, SAM SLATER.
> THE GUNFIGHTS THAT KILLED THE TWO
> MEN TOOK PLACE
> RIGHT HERE IN RISCO.

"This is going to make our town very famous," someone said, and when Sam looked around, he saw the young boy who had stabled his horse for him the night before. "Of course, everyone knows that Sims wasn't really killed here, but we have his body and the sheriff says that is the same thing."

"Is that what everyone thinks?" Sam asked. "That this is going to make Risco famous?"

"Yes. The sheriff said that now everyone will come to see where the gunfights happened. They'll buy drinks and meals in the saloon and they'll stay in the hotel. The sheriff says everyone will get rich because of this."

"And that's what all this is about? This parade and picnic?"

"Yes," the boy replied. "The sheriff says we'll have such a celebration every year at this time. It would be nice if you could come every year."

"Sure. And maybe I could kill someone new for you next year," Sam suggested.

"Do you think so? That would really be good," the boy said enthusiastically, not picking up on Sam's sarcasm.

Sam shook his head slowly, then started toward the stable. The sooner he could get out of this town, the better.

"For you, Mr. Slater, there is no charge," the liveryman said when Sam reclaimed his horse. "You have made our town famous."

"Yeah, so I noticed," Sam growled.

"You're always welcome here, Mr. Slater," the liveryman called as Sam rode away. Sam didn't answer.

Sam didn't enjoy killing, but it wasn't something he backed away from. In any life-or-death confrontation, he knew he must be prepared to kill without hesitation if need be.

There had been strong reactions to his killing before. Friends or close relatives of his victims had sworn revenge, and more than one of them had come close to carrying out their vow. And though, as a bounty hunter, Sam was always acting within the guidelines of the law, those guidelines were so thinly drawn that sometimes, a misunderstanding of his role put him afoul of the law. On more than one occasion he had nearly fallen victim to the same law he was serving, when an overzealous peace officer would charge him with murder. He was, in fact, still a wanted man in some parts of the West, including one old, still-outstanding warrant from Montana, where, on one terrible night, he had fought his drunken uncle, the same uncle who had nearly enslaved him, to keep the man from raping his own daughter. It was during that fight that Sam got the purple scar that would mark him for life. It was during that fight, also, that Sam killed his first man. That man was his uncle, and Sam had killed him in self-defense. Even so, a warrant was issued, charging Sam with murder, and Sam knew that he could never go back and make the authorities believe what really happened.

Sam left home on the run and he had been on the run ever since. He lived with the Apaches long enough to adapt himself to their ways, even to being adopted as a blood brother by some of the Apache leaders. He was born with courage and a fierce will. From his blood brothers he learned scouting, tracking, and surviving. Those were exactly the skills that would serve him well in his chosen field of bounty hunter. His phenomenal success in his chosen profession had earned him the reputation that now honored, and sometimes plagued, him.

In Sam's trade, he had received expressions of gratitude before. This was especially true in the case of relatives of the victims the outlaws

Sam encountered. But never before had an entire town put his victims on public display and thrown a town party to celebrate. It was more than he could stomach, and he couldn't wait to shake the dust of this town from his feet. As soon as he was out of Risco, he put his horse into a ground-eating lope, placing as much distance behind him as he could.

SALCEDO WAS A SMALL TOWN, JUST AS LUCAS Babbit had said. However, because it was the only town within a radius of fifty miles, it was a busy town, and half a dozen wagons were parked along the streets. The board sidewalks were full of men and women, farmers and ranchers, looking in the windows of the shops, hurrying to and fro.

"What the hell?" Charley said, surprised by the number of people. Is this Saturday?"

"I don't know. I don't keep no calendar," Babbit answered.

"There's an awful lot of people in town, Charley," Purcell said. "Maybe too many."

"Yeah?" Billy answered. "Well, look at 'em. Most of 'em ain't wearin' guns. Don't worry about it."

"There's the bank over there," Babbit pointed out.

The bank was a rather flimsy-looking building, thrown together from ripsawed lumber and leaning so that it looked as if a good, stiff wind would knock it over. Billy chuckled when he saw it.

"Hell, we don't have to rob this bank, boys. We can just kick it down," he said.

"Let's do it and be gone," Babbit suggested.

"Wait a minute, wait a minute," Charley said, holding up his hand. "Let's take a ride up and down the street first, just to get our bearings."

"Good idea," Purcell said, breathing a sigh of relief.

"Billy, you take the left side. Count everybody you see carryin' a gun. Lucas, you take the right."

The three men rode slowly down the entire length of the town, then they turned their horses and rode back.

"I seen three that was wearin' guns," Purcell said.

"I only seen one on my side," Babbit added.

"Any of them look like they knew how to use them?"

"The old fart on my side looked like he didn't even have the strength to pull his gun out of the holster, let alone use it," Babbit said.

"Billy?"

"No," Purcell answered. "They didn't any of 'em look like they knew much more'n which end of the gun the bullet come out."

Charley smiled. "Well, then, boys, let's go get us a little travelin' money. Billy, you stay outside with the horses."

Charley and Babbit swung down from their horses and handed the reins over to Purcell, who stayed mounted. He held the reins of all three horses with his left hand while in his right he held his pistol, though he kept it low and out of sight.

As soon as Charley and Babbit were inside, they pulled their pistols.

"This is a holdup!" Charley shouted. "You, teller, empty out your bank drawer and put all the money in a bag!"

Nervously the teller began to comply, emptying his drawer in just a few seconds.

"Is that all there is? There can't be more'n a couple hundred there," Charley said in disbelief.

"That's all there is," the teller insisted.

Charley took the sack. "I want to see what you've got in the safe," he demanded.

"The hell you say! You ain't gettin' any more money from this bank!" a customer suddenly shouted. Charley swung his gun toward the customer, who was also armed. The customer fired first. His bullet hit an inkwell on one of the tables, sending up a spray of ink. Charley returned fire and his bullet found its mark. Lucas fired toward the teller's window and his bullet shattered the shaded glass around the teller cages. Another customer in the bank fired and Babbit returned fire, killing him.

"Let's get the hell out of here!" Charley shouted.

Outside the bank the townspeople, hearing the shots, realized at once what was going on.

"The bank!" someone shouted. "They're robbin' the bank!"

"Charley, Lucas!" Purcell shouted. "Get out of there! Fast!"

One of the armed townspeople started running toward the bank with his pistol drawn. Purcell shot him, dropping him in the middle of the street. Until that moment not everyone realized that Purcell, too, was one of the bank robbers. Seeing that he was one of them, the townspeople began screaming and running for cover.

Clutching the canvas bag in his left hand, Charley and Babbit backed out of the bank. Babbit fired three more shots into the bank, knocking out the windows on both sides and in the door.

"Get mounted!" Purcell called, holding the reins down for his two partners.

Across the street a young store clerk, no more than a boy, came running out of the store, wearing his apron and carrying a broom in one hand and a rifle in the other. He dropped the broom, raised the rifle, and fired at the three robbers. His bullet hit Purcell in the side, and with a roar of pain and anger, Purcell fired back, killing the boy. From the front porch of a hardware store, a man fired both barrels of a shotgun, but his gun was loaded with light birdshot and he was too far away to be effective. The pellets peppered and stung, but none of them penetrated the skin.

Babbit grabbed the horse nearest him and swung into the saddle. When the owner ... ped out the door of a nearby shop to pr... it shot at him, and the bullet ... r frame right beside the m... back inside.

The sheriff ... described h... havin... t...

man's skull, carrying with it a little spray of blood, bone, and brain matter.

The three robbers rode toward the end of town only to see a dozen or more of the townspeople rolling a wagon into the street. The townspeople then tipped the wagon over as a barricade and gathered behind it, all of them armed and ready.

"Charley, we can't go that way!" Purcell shouted.

"This way!" Charley yelled, turning off the street and leading them through a churchyard where a funeral was in progress and the body was just being carried from the church.

At the sound of gunfire and the sight of three mounted and armed men bearing down on them, the funeral procession broke up amid screams and shouts of terror and outrage. The pallbearers dropped the coffin and the lid popped off, allowing the last remains of a bearded old man to roll out.

By the time the townspeople regrouped and mounted, Charley Harris, Billy Purcell, and Lucas Babbit had a two-mile lead on them. With the eriff dead and no effective leader to organize the pursuit only lasted for a few miles. After gave up and came back to town to bury the dead.

"They've stopped chasin' us," Charley said, looking back over his shoulder. "We can give the animals a blow now."

The three riders reined up, then swung down from their saddles and began walking their horses. Purcell, who had been hit in the hip, was walking with a painful limp. There was blood on the front of his trousers.

"You bad hit, pard?" Charley asked solicitously.

"No."

"You sure? You're covered with blood and you got a pretty bad hitch-along in your get-about there."

"I ain't hurt bad," Purcell insisted. "I got a bullet in my hip, but it didn't hit none of my vitals."

"Yeah, well, we can't leave the bullet in there," Charley said. "We'll have to get you to a doctor somewhere."

"No!" Purcell shouted. "I seen how you got a doctor for Barnett. I ain't plannin' on lettin' you leave me somewhere to die."

"That was different," Charley said. "We was on the run then."

"Well, what the hell, Charley? We ain't exactly goin' to a ball now."

Charley and Babbit laughed.

"That's the truth," Charley said. "All right, if you think you can keep up with us, go ahead. But you start slowin' us down any, we're goin' to leave you."

"I didn't figure it would be any otherwise," Purcell replied.

"You want, I can get that bullet out for you," Babbit offered.

"You a doctor, are you?"

"I've took out a few bullets in my day," Babbit said. "And some of 'em lived."

"I'll pass on that offer, but thanks just the same," Purcell said.

Despite Purcell's brave protestations, by nightfall the pain was almost unbearable and he knew he wouldn't be able to go on unless the bullet was removed. He finally spoke the words.

"Lucas," he said thickly. "You serious 'bout bein' able to take out a bullet?"

Babbit chuckled. "You ready for it to come out now, are you?"

"Yes."

"I thought you would be. I've heard 'em talk brave before, but most always they change their mind. I'll take it out for you."

"Thanks."

"It's goin' to cost you."

"Cost me? Cost me what?"

"Your share of the money we took from the bank."

"Are you crazy? I got shot for that money. You think I'm goin' to give it to you?"

"Don't look to me like you got no choice,"

Babbit said. "Anyhow, what's the big deal. We only got a hundred fifty dollars. Your share's just fifty bucks."

"Who would've thought they would put up such a fight for just a hundred fifty dollars?" Purcell asked. "Four men killed, me wounded, all for a lousy hundred fifty dollars."

"Do we have a deal?" Babbit asked.

At that very moment a wave of nauseating pain swept over Purcell with such intensity that it was all he could do to stay in the saddle. "All right, you bastard, all right, we have a deal. You can have my share, just get the damn bullet out," Purcell said in a strained voice.

"I know this country, Charley," Babbit said. "Head up into that draw over there. That'll take us into Snake Canyon."

"Good," Charley said. "Maybe we can hole up for a while."

"We're goin' to hole up?" Purcell asked.

"That's right, Billy, we're goin' to hole up," Charley said. He chuckled. "Did you really think we was goin' to leave you?"

"I don't know," Purcell answered. "Yeah, I guess I thought you might."

"Well, we ain't. We're the only ones left now. That means we got to stick together. Besides, what would folks think of Cactus Charley if they knew he abandoned his friends?"

"Yeah," Purcell replied, thinking of Ray

Barnett, Kelly Sims, and Jeb Scruggs. "Yeah, what would they think of you?"

It was another hour of painful riding before they stopped. Purcell climbed down from his horse, removed the saddle, then lay down, using it as a pillow. The pain, which had been localized in his hip, now spread throughout both legs and up his back.

"We need to build us a fire," Babbit said.

"Kind of hate to," Charley said. "You can see a fire a long way off at night. Somebody might see this and get to wonderin' who's out here."

"We got to have a fire for me to heat the knife," Babbit said.

There was the double, metallic click of a pistol being cocked, and when Babbit and Charley looked around, they saw that Purcell was pointing his gun at Charley.

"Let him build a fire, Charley," Purcell said through clenched teeth. "Else he'll have to be takin' a bullet outta both of us."

"Sure, Billy, sure," Charley said, holding his hands up. "I didn't say we wasn't goin' to build one. I was just pointin' out that we needed to be extra careful, that's all. Go ahead, Lucas, build your fire."

Purcell, no longer having to fight to stay alert and in the saddle, drifted in and out of consciousness. He was aware of Lucas Babbit gathering bits of mesquite wood, but he didn't see him actually start the fire. He saw the golden bubble of light in the night, with Charley and Babbit silhouetted against the flames, then he passed out again.

He woke up again when Babbit started actually digging for the bullet. The pain was excruciating, much more intense than it had been at any time before. He passed out again. When he came to the next time, Babbit was holding the bloodied bullet between his fingers and smiling broadly, his eyes and teeth glowing orange red in the snapping fire.

"Can you believe this?" Babbit said. "This here is a twenty-two. Who shot you anyway, Billy? Some kid with a toy gun?"

"I don't remember," said Purcell, who, in fact, did recall at that moment the young, apron-clad boy he had killed.

"Give me three of your bullets," Babbit said.

"What? What do you want my bullets for?"

"Because I need the gunpowder," Babbit replied. "And I ain't plannin' on usin' any of my own."

"I got a box of cartridges in my saddlebag," Purcell said. He tried to reach for them but was too weak.

"I'll get 'em," Babbit offered generously. When he opened the box, he took out ten or twelve, dropping the extra cartridges into his own pocket. He came back to sit beside Purcell as he separated the bullets from the cartridges. When he had all three separated, he poured the powder on the wound.

"What's that for?" Purcell asked.

"You'll see," Babbit replied. Without a word of explanation, he picked up a burning brand from the fire and touched off the powder. It made a white-hot flash.

Purcell had time only for a gasp of pain before he passed out.

WHEN PURCELL OPENED HIS EYES THE NEXT morning, he was looking directly at the camp fire, or rather at what had been the camp fire. Now there were only a few white coals with a tiny wisp of smoke curling up from the ashes.

"Charley," he said. "Charley, could I have a drink of water?"

When no one answered, Purcell turned, with a great effort, to look around. He didn't see anyone.

"Charley? Lucas?" he shouted, the effort of the yell causing his wound to throb.

There was still no answer.

With a supreme effort Purcell sat up and

looked around. The camp was totally deserted. Not only were Charley and Babbit gone, but all three horses were as well. They had left in the night, leaving him wounded and without a mount.

"You son of a bitch!" Purcell shouted. "You bastard!" He picked up a rock and threw it, though the effort caused pain to shoot through him like a hot knife. He fell back down and lay there until the pain subsided, somewhat. The thirst he had awakened with seemed to increase with his efforts, so he reached for his canteen. When he couldn't find it on his saddle pommel, he looked around for it.

The canteen was gone. So were his saddlebags. There was jerky, raisins, and dried beans in his saddlebag. Not only had they taken his horse, they had taken his canteen and his food.

Waves of panic swept over him, pushing aside the rage and even the pain. He was abandoned out here, no horse, too wounded to walk, no food, and no water. He was going to die, a long, slow, agonizing death. Even Ray had it better than this, he thought. He had food, water, and a place to sleep, followed by a quick death.

"Shit!" he shouted into the dry, morning, wind. "I would have been better off lettin' them hang me."

Purcell saw his pistol and, in a sudden

impulse, drew it from his holster. He put the barrel to his temple.

"Charley Harris! Lucas Babbit!" he shouted. "I'll be waiting for you in hell!"

Purcell pulled the trigger.

It was that same afternoon when Sam, who had been alone on the range for the last two days and so knew nothing of Charley Harris's most recent bank robbery, pushed through the bat-wing doors of the Lucky Chance Saloon in the little town of Three Wells. It was still too early in the day for the evening trade. As a result an empty beer mug and a half-full ashtray conveniently placed by the piano provided the only evidence that anyone ever played the instrument. Sam ordered a beer, and when it was served, he turned around to survey the room as he drank it.

Two people were sitting at the table nearest the piano . . . a middle-aged cowboy and the only bargirl who was working at this hour. The fact that both of them had only one glass before them, and that glass was still half-full, indicated that the bargirl either found the cowboy's company pleasant or had accepted the slowness of the afternoon.

There were a few people sitting at one of the other tables and a lively card game was in progress. The table was crowded with brightly colored poker chips and empty beer mugs. There were two brass spittoons within spitting distance of the players, but despite their presence, the floor was riddled with expectorated tobacco quids and chewed cigar butts.

Suddenly one of the players threw his cards on the table in disgust, then stood up. "I've had it, boys," he said. "This is the unluckiest chair I've ever sat in. I ain't drawed a winnin' hand all night."

Another player looked over toward the bar and saw Sam watching them.

"We have an empty chair here, mister, if you'd care to sit in."

Sam tossed the rest of his drink down, then wiped the back of his hand across his mouth. He had learned long ago that it was sometimes easier to pick up information through casual conversation over a few drinks and a deck of cards than to ask outright. Maybe someone at the table had heard something about Harris and the others. That was justification for joining the card game, though in truth he did enjoy a good game now and then.

"Thanks for the invite," Sam said. "I will join you if you don't mind."

"What you take out of your pocket and put in front of you is all the money you can play with," one of the men said. "You can't go back for more."

"And you can't put any more in front of you than the most any of us have."

"Who's been the winner so far?"

"That'd be the doc here," one of the cowboys said. "You'd better watch out for him. He's pretty good at the game."

"Thanks for the warning. And you would be the doc?" Sam asked, addressing the man with the largest pile of money.

"I am," the tall, thin, cadaverous-looking man replied. He was wearing a black suit, a shoestring tie, and a flat-crown, black hat. He counted the money in front of him. "I've got forty-five dollars here."

Sam bought forty-five dollars' worth of chips and stacked them up in front of him.

"You just passin' through Three Wells?" the man in black asked as he dealt the cards. It was easy to see why he was ahead. He handled the cards easily, gracefully, whereas the others around the table looked awkward, even picking up the pasteboards.

"Depends," Sam answered.

"On what?" one of the other men asked.

"On how much I win here. If I win enough, I might buy a ranch and some cattle, get married, settle down, raise a family, join a church, run for the city council, and become a substantial citizen."

The men around the table laughed out loud.

"Say, Smokey," Doc called to the cowboy who was sitting with the bar girl. "Did you hear this fella? If he wins big, he's goin' to be lookin' for a wife. You better hang on to Belle while you can."

Belle looked over at Sam. "Honey, you're a good-lookin' man," she teased. "You wouldn't have to win too much to get me."

Belle's good-natured response brought more laughter.

Sam won the first hand.

"Better watch it, Doc," one of the cowboys said. "This fella's on his way."

The game continued for several hands. Sam was winning a little more than he was losing, but he wasn't the big winner. Neither was the one called Doc at this point, the play of Sam changing the dynamics to the point where everyone seemed to be about even. This had the effect of improving everyone's mood and the talk came freely. Besides Dr. Shelby, who was a real doctor in addition to being an almost professional gambler, the other men in the game were Mitch McCoy, a small rancher, Marcus Feeler, a leathersmith, and Andy Potter, who owned the feed-and-seed store.

"Say," Sam said as if merely taking part in the conversation, "did any of you fellas hear about the big jailbreak they had over in Gunther a few weeks ago?"

"Jailbreak? Mister, that's old news. Where

you been?" Mitch replied. "Hell, yesterday Charley Harris and his boys done robbed 'em a bank over in Salcedo."

"Some bank robbery," Marcus said in disgust. "They only made off with one hundred and fifty dollars."

"They didn't get much money, that's true," Andy agreed. "But they killed four people doin' it. One of 'em was just a boy."

"A boy?" Doc asked. "What boy? I've doctored a few of the young'uns over there."

"It was Muley Simpson's boy," Andy replied. "Muley runs the general store there, you know, and his boy was workin' for him. Seems the boy had just got hisself a new twenty-two rifle, an' when all the shootin' started, why, he run out onto the front porch an' joined in the melee. They say he hit one of 'em, though they might just be sayin' that to ease Muley's pain some. Whether he actual did hit one of them or not, he got their attention, 'cause he was shot dead, right there on the front porch of his pa's store."

"That's a damned shame. It's too bad they didn't get all them fellas hung when they had the chance," Marcus said. "I wonder where they are now?"

"Say, you know, I was talkin' to one of my nighthawks this mornin'," Mitch said. "Well, it was Pete Malloy, you fellas all know him. Anyhow, I was talkin' to him an' he said that last night he thought he saw a camp fire down in Snake Canyon. I didn't put much store in it at the time, but now that I think back on it, don't it seem to you a little curious? I mean why would anyone want to go in there? The place is so desolate that a hawk has to carry a lunch just to fly over."

The others laughed.

"Snake Canyon, eh?" Marcus said. "You think maybe Charley Harris and his bunch is holed up there?"

"Well, if I was on the run, that's sure where I'd go," Mitch said. "Why, they's enough draws and gullies in that place to hide a whole army."

As the evening progressed several more people came in, until eventually the saloon was noisy and crowded with its evening customers. Three of the most noticeable of the newly arrived customers were young men who wore their guns strapped low. They were louder and more boisterous than anyone else in the establishment, and they made a place for themselves at the bar by elbowing others out of the way. Occasionally one of them would get off a joke at someone else's expense, and he and the other two would laugh uproariously at his cleverness, unaware, or unconcerned, that the rest of the people in the saloon were not laughing with them, but were, instead, taking it all in, in embarrassed silence.

"Who are the funny boys?" Sam finally asked.

"The one with blond hair and the loudest mouth is Mel Butrum. He's the oldest. The one with the red hair is Willie Cole. The one with the dark hair and moustache is Eddie Webber. They rode for me once, till I got rid of them. Then they rode for first one rancher then another, 'till one by one ever'one got sick of 'em. I guess they been fired by ever' spread within fifty miles. Now they mostly drift about, rounding up a few strays for their money."

"Yeah, and sometimes the strays ain't even strayed yet," Doc said. "What gets me is why you ranchers don't know that."

"We know it," Mitch admitted. "But we figure payin' a few bucks to get our strays back is better'n havin' 'em rustled."

"They're a rowdy bunch of bullies, all right," Doc said. "Don't nobody like 'em. In fact, I'm a little surprised to see them. They got drunk here two, maybe three weeks ago and tore up the place. Sheriff Pratt told them they was either goin' to have to pay for the damages or spend thirty days in jail."

"Which did they do?" Sam asked.

"Hell, they didn't do neither one," Doc replied. "They just lit out. This is the first time they've been back since."

"I wonder if the sheriff knows they're in town?" Marcus asked.

The three men who were the subject of the

table conversation, perhaps sensing that they were being talked about, left the bar and wandered over to the card game.

"Well, now, this here looks like a friendly game," one of them said. This was Mel. "Any of you 'bout ready to give up your seats?"

No one answered.

"Hey, you, Scarface," Mel said to Sam. Willie and Eddie laughed. "Why don't you take a rest for a while and let one of us sit in the game?"

"Hey, Mel, you want to play, you go right ahead," Willie said. "I didn't come into town to play no cards. Hell, we can do that out at the bunkhouse. I come for somethin' else."

"Yeah, Willie, we know what you come for," Eddie said. "You come to dip your wick."

The three men found that enormously funny.

"So, how 'bout it, Scarface? You goin' to get up, or what?" Willie asked.

"I'm not ready to quit yet," Sam said.

"Is that so? Well, maybe if you'd win one big hand, you'd be ready," Mel suggested. "I'll help you." He started walking around the table. "Doc here has hisself a pair of jacks," he said. "Mitch is holdin' a king, queen, and ace, but no pair." He stepped behind the leatherworker's chair. "Whoooee. Now, Marcus has two kings." He looked up. "Hope you can beat two kings."

Doc, Mitch, and Marcus groaned, and Sam put his cards, down, faceup, on the table. He had two aces. "What do you say we leave the pot and redeal?" he suggested to the others.

"Thanks. That's damned decent of you," Doc said.

"Hold it now, that's no way to be. I'm just trying to help."

Sam glared at the young cowboy. "I've had a bellyfull of you, mister," he said. "Back away from the table."

Sam's words were cold and clipped, and the easy banter fell away from the three young men. Mel licked his lips, the tip of his tongue darting out, snakelike.

"What did you say to me?"

"I told you to back away from the table."

"Mister, you don't think you can make words like that stick, do you?"

"I reckon I can."

"I don't know why I'm wastin' my time explainin' things to a scar-faced, dried-up bastard like you. Maybe I'm just an all-around nice guy. But someone ought to tell you that when you're sittin' down and I'm standin' up, there's no way you can get a gun out faster'n me. Now, you goin' to back up them words? Or you goin' to eat 'em?"

"I reckon I'll back 'em up," Sam said. During the entire confrontation one of his hands had been under the table. Now he brought it above the table and everyone gasped, because he was holding a Colt .44. Sam moved his lips into what could be called a smile, though the smile didn't quite reach the cold glint of his steel-blue eyes. "Looks like I did get it out faster, doesn't it? Now, you can try me, or you can go on about your business and leave us to ours."

The expression on the young cowboy's face changed from one of cockiness to fear. He put both hands up and started backing away.

"Listen, listen, mister," he said. "I didn't mean nothin' by all this. I was just funnin', that's all. You boys go on now and enjoy your game."

"We intend to," Sam said.

The three cowboys walked away from the table.

Doc laughed. "Mister, if you won every hand for the rest of the night, it would be worth it," he said. "I've been wanting to see somebody stand up to those boys for a long time."

THE THREE COWBOYS, AFTER LEAVING THE game table, returned to the bar for another drink. They were a bit more subdued than they had been when they first came in. Mel began drinking hard, tossing down one whiskey after another, while Willie and Eddie tried to calm him down. Finally Willie and Eddie gave up and left Mel to brood while they walked over to the table occupied by Smokey and Belle. Belle had stayed with Smokey, even though business had improved and it would have been much more profitable for her to leave him and begin working the crowd.

"Hello, Belle," Willie said.

Belle looked at him, then turned back to talk to Smokey.

"Hey, Willie, what do you think? It looks like Belle don't love you no more," Eddie suggested.

"Yeah? Well, we'll see about that," Willie retorted. "Look here, you old fart," he said to Smokey. "If you ain't goin' to take Belle up to her room, then quit chewin' her ears off and let someone do it who's still young enough to get the job done."

Smokey turned in his chair and looked up at Willie. "You go ahead, sonny," he said. "Take her upstairs. I'll still be here when she's finished."

"Go ahead, Willie. You got his permission," Eddie teased.

"Yeah, well, I don't need the son of a bitch's permission," Willie replied. He reached down to grab Belle's arm and she had to stand quickly to keep him from pulling her to her feet. "Tell you what, Eddie. Why don't you go back over there and have a drink with Mel? This here ain't goin' to take very long."

Smokey chuckled. "No," he said. "I don't reckon it will."

"What's that s'posed to mean?" Willie growled.

"Why, it don't mean nothin' at all, Willie," Smokey said. "I was just makin' conversation, that's all."

Willie laughed, a high-pitched laugh. "Yeah, well, seem's that's 'bout all you're good for," he said. Tugging roughly on Belle's arm, he pulled her over to the stairs, then up to the second floor.

"I feel sorry for the girl," Marcus said.

Doc looked up. "Yeah, well, don't worry none about Belle. She's had plenty of experience handling people like that."

Though Sam said nothing, he tended to agree with Doc. He didn't like to see any woman, even a soiled dove, mistreated, but it had been his observation over the years that women like Belle were pretty good at protecting themselves.

Sam lost the redealt hand, then pushed himself away from the table. "I appreciate the game, gentlemen," he said. "But I think I'll just have a drink or two, then call it a night. Thanks for letting me sit in."

"We enjoyed your company, mister. New blood's always welcome, if it's friendly," Doc said. "What about it, Marcus? Redeal?"

"Not for me, thanks," Marcus replied. "I think I'll call it a night, too."

"Me, too," Mitch added. "We may as well break up the game now, or Mel will be over here again, wantin' to play."

"Yeah, I'll go along with that," Andy said.

"You fellas can quit if you want to, but I'd like to get the winning edge back," Doc said.

"There are a couple of other games going on now. I think I'll see if I can join one of them."

Sam said good-bye to his friends, then walked over to the bar and ordered a drink. He had taken only one sip when the bat-wing doors swung open and a man, wearing a badge, stepped into the saloon.

"It's Sheriff Pratt," someone said.

"Smoke's goin' to fly now, fellas," another put in. "He done give them three boys the word not to come back to town till they paid off the damages."

"Mel Butrum," Sheriff Pratt called.

"Hello, Pratt. What got you away from your coffee and your nice, cushioned chair?"

"I smelled a stink in the air and I figured you was over here," Sheriff Pratt replied. "Did you bring one hundred dollars to cover the damages you caused the other night?"

"I told you I wasn't goin' to pay for them damages," Mel said without turning around.

"Then I reckon you'll be spendin' some time in jail."

Mel and Eddie both turned toward the sheriff. Mel smiled evilly at him.

"I don't reckon I'd care to do that, Pratt," Mel said. "You see, I'm pretty much what you'd call an outdoors man. Gettin' locked up in a jail ain't for me."

Sheriff Pratt held out his hand. "Give me your gun, Mel," he said. "You, too, Eddie."

Mel shook his head, the evil smile still pasted across his mouth.

"You want our guns, Sheriff, you're goin' to have to take 'em away from us. That is, if you think you're able to do it."

At Mel's challenging words, there was a sudden frenzied movement as people in the line of fire hurried to get out of the way. Only Mel and Eddie remained at the bar. Even Sam moved to the far end to be out of the way of any wild shot that might happen, should shooting break out.

"It doesn't have to be this way, boys," the sheriff said. "A few broken windows and chairs? It hardly seems worth dyin' over."

"That all depends on who's goin' to be dyin'," Mel said, moving his hand in position just over the handle of his pistol. "You see, the way I'm figurin' is, you're the one that's goin' to do the dyin'."

Sam was a little surprised by Mel's bravado. He had already proven himself to be a braggart and a loudmouth, but when it came right down to it, braggarts and loudmouths usually caved in to calm courage. And this sheriff had already impressed Sam with the fact that he was a no-nonsense man of courage. What, then, was giving Mel his edge?

Sam sensed, more than saw or heard, the movement at the top of the stairs. When he looked up, he saw Willie, aiming at the sheriff.

So, this was why Mel was so confident. He knew that Willie was upstairs with the drop on the sheriff, while the sheriff had no idea of the additional threat.

Ordinarily Sam never interfered in another man's fight. There were many reasons why he stayed out of them. Most of the time people resented interference, even if it had been undertaken with the best of intentions. Other times he just didn't know which side to back. This time, however, he had no problem with that. He had met the three cowboys and already disliked them enough to be partial to anyone who might be opposed to them. As it turned out, that was all the justification he needed to give the warning.

"Sheriff, there's a man on the landing with the drop on you," Sam warned loudly.

Angry that his ambush plans were spoiled by Sam's yell, Willie turned his gun on Sam.

"You scar-faced son of a bitch!" he shouted, pulling the trigger even as he yelled.

Sam jumped to one side, pulling his pistol and shooting, almost as quickly as Willie. The slug that Willie fired from the balcony missed Sam and slammed into the glass mirror behind the bar. The mirror shattered and fell, leaving only a few jagged shards hanging in place to reflect, in distorted images, the scene playing before it.

Willie didn't get away a second shot because Sam had fired right on top of him, and Sam's bullet found it's mark. Willie dropped his pistol and grabbed his throat, then stood there, clutching his neck, as blood oozed between his fingers. Then his eyes rolled up into his head and he twisted and fell, sliding headfirst down the stairs and following his clattering pistol all the way to the bottom. He lay motionless on the lowest step, his open but sightless eyes staring vacantly at the ceiling.

At the same time as Sam and Willie were having their shoot-out, Mel and the sheriff had also joined in the ball. Sam was still watching Willie slide down the stairs when he heard the roar of two more Colts. Though it seemed to him that time had stilled, thus causing a great separation between his and Willie's shots, and the next two shots, the truth was that the battle between Mel and the sheriff had taken place almost simultaneously with his own fight.

Mel had fired at the sheriff first, but his shot was badly placed. All it did was put a hole in the sheriff's hat. The sheriff's shot hit Mel in the forehead and Mel slid down to the floor in the sitting position, his body held up by the bar, his hands lying on the floor to each side of him. Like Willie, Mel had been killed instantly.

"No, no, don't shoot! Don't shoot!" Eddie

shouted, holding his hands up in the air. "I ain't in this fight! I ain't in this fight!"

"Shuck your belt," the sheriff ordered.

"I'm doin' it, I'm doin' it," Eddie said, using his left hand to unfasten his belt buckle. The gun belt dropped to the floor with a clatter.

The sheriff looked at Eddie for a long moment, and Sam could almost believe he was going to shoot anyway. Finally he sighed and made a waving motion with his pistol.

"Get out of here, Eddie," the sheriff said. "Just thank God you got out of here alive. Leave town and don't ever come back."

"But Mel and Willie," Eddie said, taking in the two dead bodies with a sweep of his arm.

"We'll take care of the dead," the sheriff promised. "Now, if you don't want to wind up in jail for a very long time . . . get out of here."

"I'm goin', I'm goin'," Eddie said, starting for the door.

The sheriff looked toward Sam, then put his pistol away. Sam did the same.

"I owe you my thanks, mister," he said.

"Yeah, well, I didn't plan to get involved," Sam said. "But he didn't leave me much choice."

The sheriff looked at Sam, then up toward the top of the stairs where Willie had been standing, then back to Sam. "That's a pretty good shot, Mister," he said. "You know, I'd make that better'n sixty feet. Would you agree?"

"That's as good a guess as any," Sam said.

"It's seventy-five feet if it's an inch," Doc insisted. He had gone over to Willie and was now examining the cowboy's wound. He didn't need to examine Mel. With a hole in his forehead, his eyes wide open and opaque, and in the sitting position, leaning back against the bar, Mel was very obviously dead. "Seventy-five feet," Doc added, "and the bullet caught old Willie-boy here right in the windpipe. Yes, sir, I'd say that was one hell of a shot."

The sheriff looked more closely at Sam. "Say, I know you, don't I?"

"I don't believe we've had the pleasure," Sam replied.

"You're right, we've never met in person," the sheriff agreed. He shook his finger slightly as he pointed it at Sam. But there's no need for us to have met for me to know who you are. I've heard enough stories about you that I ought to have recognized you on sight. If that big purple scar on your cheekbone there wasn't enough, why, there was also the way you handled that pistol. No, sir, you can't be no one else but the fella they call the Regulator. Am I right?"

"I prefer to be called Sam."

Sheriff Pratt snapped his fingers and smiled broadly. "I'm right, aren't I? I knew I was right." He looked at the two bodies, which had now been picked up and laid out, side by, side, on one of the longer tables. "Is there paper out on these boys? If so, I wasn't aware of it."

"I wasn't after them," Sam replied. "They just happened to get in the way."

"Who are you after?"

"I think I can tell you that," Doc volunteered.

"Oh? And who would that be?" the sheriff asked.

"Unless I miss my guess, he's after Charley Harris," Mitch suggested to the sheriff. Then he looked directly at Sam. "That was pretty slick of you, Sam, to get into a card game with us just so you could get information," he added.

"I've learned that sometimes it's better to take the long way around," Sam explained.

"I guess that's right most of the time," Mitch replied. "But the truth is, there isn't a man here who doesn't want to see Charley Harris and that bunch get their due. In case you missed what we were saying a while ago, a fire down in Snake Canyon this time of year is awfully curious."

Pratt chuckled. "Mitch, do you know you're givin' away information there that's worth fifteen hundred dollars?"

"Fifteen hundred dollars? How do you figure?" Mitch asked.

"There's five hundred dollars' reward money out on Charley Harris, Billy Purcell, and Kelly Sims," he said.

"Not Kelly Sims," Sam interjected.

"Yeah, him, too," the sheriff insisted. "He's worth as much as either one of the other two fellas."

"I've already collected on Sims," Sam said matter-of-factly.

"When did you get him? The word we got was there was three men held up the bank over in Salcedo yesterday."

"That was Harris, Purcell, and Babbit. Lucas Babbit," Sam said. "Babbit is one of the two men who helped the three escape."

"What about the other man who helped them?" the sheriff asked. "Who is he?"

"Jeb Scruggs," Sam replied easily.

"Jeb Scruggs," the sheriff repeated. He shook his head. "You know, I don't recall even seein' a poster on that gentlemen. If he comes through here, I won't even know him."

"Don't worry about him," Sam said easily.

"Well, I'd at least like to know if he—" The sheriff stopped in midsentence. "You got him, too, didn't you?"

"Yesterday afternoon."

"You're a busy man, Mr. Slater."

"I try to do my job, Sheriff Pratt."

"Who is this Lucas Babbit, Pratt?" Doc asked. "Have you ever heard of him?"

"Yes, I've heard of him," Pratt answered. "He's a mean one, all right. Maybe even meaner than the others."

"As far as I'm concerned, any money Sam Slater gets from handling people like Harris and Babbit and the others, he's entitled to. Believe me, I have no interest in trying to collect any of it for myself." Mitch looked at Sam. "So, if the knowledge that Harris and his bunch may be poking around down in Snake Canyon is useful to you, have it, and have it with my blessing."

"Thanks," Sam said. "I reckon I'll be checking that place out."

Sam's weren't the only ears to hear the possible location of Charley Harris. Eddie Webber had been run out of the saloon a few minutes earlier by the sheriff, but he hadn't actually gone anywhere. Right now he was standing in the shadows by the bat-wing doors just outside the saloon. With his back to the wall and a small, two-shot sleeve gun cradled in his raised, right hand, Eddie planned to shoot Sam the moment he stepped outside.

As he listened, however, he began to have other plans. If Harris and his gang were worth that much money to Sam Slater . . . how much money would Slater be worth to them?

Pete Malloy wasn't the only one who had seen the camp fire last night. Eddie, Willie, and Mel had seen it, too. And not only did Eddie know where it was, he knew a shorter way to get there. If he could get to Charley Harris and his gang before Slater and provide them with information as to when and where Sam Slater would come for them, they would be mighty grateful. They might even let him join them.

EDDIE WAS PRETTY DEEP INTO THE CANYON at the mouth of McKenzie Draw. Though there were literally dozens of draws and gullies in the canyon that would offer shelter, McKenzie Draw was the only one that offered a way back out. When Eddie stopped just outside the mouth of the draw, he climbed up onto a protruding finger and looked over into it.

It was too dark to see anything, so he decided to wait until dawn. There were three of them and only one of him, and he had no desire to stumble into their camp in the middle of the night. That would be a good way to get himself killed.

When Eddie looked to the east, he could see a faint streak of pearl gray. It wouldn't be much longer until it was light enough for him to approach. He could afford to wait it out. If they would listen to him, and believe him, they would still have time to prepare an ambush for Slater.

Eddie pulled a strip of jerky from his saddlebag, chewed off a piece, then wrapped what remained in the soiled and greasy waxed paper he kept it in. He chewed it for several minutes and it seemed to get bigger and bigger in his mouth. He wanted to spit it out, but he figured he would need the sustenance, so he continued to work at it. He finally managed to get the last bit down, then he followed that with a swallow of water. He wished it was coffee, but he knew that starting a fire would be foolish . . . perhaps even fatal.

The night finally lifted, illuminating the canyon floor in a soft, coral light, though lingering shadows still hung in the corners and edges of the deeper draws. Eddie climbed up to the top of the protruding finger and looked down into McKenzie Draw once more. This time he saw the camp, but he was surprised to see that there was only one person there. He knew there were at least three of them. Where were the other two?

"Oh, you clever bastards," he said quietly. "You're keeping two men on watch while one sleeps. That way nobody can sneak in on you."

He wondered, though, why they had not yet come in. He also wondered why the lone man in camp had not built a fire for their morning coffee. Maybe they were being cautious. Why weren't they that cautious the other night? Every nighthawk within twenty miles had seen the fire then.

Eddie chuckled to himself as he thought of an old saying. He said it aloud. "You boys have done shut the barn door after the horse is gone," he said.

Eddie stood up, brushed his hands together, then started walking down the other side of the little hill into the campsite.

"Hello the camp!" he called, holding his arms out so that anyone watching could clearly see that he wasn't carrying a weapon. "Hello the camp! I'm a friend!"

The two lookouts didn't come in, nor did they even make their presence known.

"Mr. Harris?" Eddie called. "Charley Harris? My name is Eddie Webber. I've come to join you, if I may."

Still no answer or movement. Even the one person in the camp was still.

"Listen, I want to warn you. The fella they call the Regulator is on his way out here. Someone give him some information that you were out here. It wasn't me," he added. "I swear, it wasn't me. I just overheard which is how come I'm here."

Eddie was beginning to get a little disconcerted. Neither of the two lookouts had given any indication as to their presence, and even the lone man in the camp was quiet.

"Mister, are you asleep? You can't be asleep. Hell, I've made more noise than a herd of cows comin' into this camp." By now Eddie was right over the supine figure, and he squatted down to touch him on the shoulder. "What's the matter with you?"

The man on the ground suddenly rolled over. Eddie saw a flash of movement, then felt the barrel of the man's pistol under his chin. He heard the hammer being cocked.

"Who are you?" the man asked.

"Eddie Webber, Eddie Webber," Eddie said in fright, backing away so quickly that he fell on his back. "Don't shoot! Don't shoot!"

The man sat up, though it seemed to be with some effort. He held his gun leveled toward Eddie. "What are you doing here?" he asked.

"I came to warn you and the others about Slater. You know, the one they call the Regulator?"

The man with the gun laughed, then he winced with pain and put his hand down to his hip. That was when Eddie saw that his right pants leg was caked with dried blood.

"You're hurt?" he asked.

"Yeah. Some kid shot me with a twenty-two."

He laughed again, a dry, brittle laugh. "Can you believe that? Billy Purcell gettin' shot by a kid? With a twenty-two?"

"You're Billy Purcell?"

"Yeah, that's me." Purcell squinted at Eddie. "Who'd you say you were again?"

"My name is Eddie, Mr. Purcell. Eddie Webber."

"What are you doin' out here, Eddie?"

"Like I told you, I came to warn you about Slater."

"Why would you do that?"

"Well, for one thing, I don't like the son of a bitch very much," Eddie said. "He killed one of my friends yesterday. And for another, I thought maybe you and Mr. Harris and Mr. Babbit would let me join up with you."

Purcell laughed again, another dry, brittle, laugh. "You want to ride the outlaw trail do you, Eddie?" he asked.

"Yes."

"You're bold and brave and you want to join that gallant band of brothers whose home is the wind and whose destiny is danger?"

"What?"

Purcell laughed heartily. "I got that from one of those dime novels some fool wrote about Charley. Charley carries them with him, you know, and if he finds somebody who hasn't heard of him, he shows them the books."

"I never knew they wrote no books about Charley Harris."

"You've never heard of Cactus Charley?"

"I've heard of Charley Harris," Eddie said. "I never heard him called Cactus Charley."

Purcell laughed again. "Charley won't like that," he said. "He sets a great store by those dime novels."

Eddie looked around nervously.

"Where is he?" he asked. "I thought there were three of you. Are the others standing watch?"

"Yeah, they're standing watch," Purcell said. "By now they're watching the whores dance in Aquilla."

"Aquilla? That's a hundred miles south of here, near to the border."

"That's the general idea," Purcell replied.

"But what are you doin' here?" Eddie looked around the campsite. "Where's your horse?"

"You noticed that, did you? My horse is gone. They took it with them . . . along with my share of the money from the bank job in Salcedo, and my water and my food. If the bastards could've turned me in for the five-hundred-dollar reward money, they would've done that, too. You got any water?"

"Yeah. My canteen's on the horse. Why did they leave you here like this?"

"They thought I'd slow 'em down," Purcell said. "Get me some water, will you?"

"Sure," Eddie said. He went back for his horse, and as he was loosing the hobble he saw a plume of dust in the distance, glowing brightly in the early morning sun. He hurried his horse back into the camp. "Someone's coming," he said.

"Slater?"

"It has to be," Eddie replied. He handed his canteen to Purcell, who, thirstily, took several long, swallows. "Easy, it's ten miles to the nearest water hole."

Purcell handed the canteen back to Eddie. "Thanks," he said.

"What are we going to do about Slater?" Eddie asked.

"You got a rifle?"

"Yeah, I have a rifle."

"Tell you what you do. You tie your horse here, then you take your rifle and go over there, in those rocks, and wait. I'll be the bait, you see. And when Slater comes into the camp, you'll have a perfect bead on him."

"Yeah," Eddie said. "Yeah, that's a good idea."

"Leave me your pistol," Purcell said.

"What?"

"Leave me your pistol."

"What do you want with my pistol?"

"That's a thirty-seven, isn't it?"

"Yes."

"Mine's a forty-four. I don't have no bullets and what you got won't fit mine."

"You don't have any shells at all?"

"None," Billy replied. He thought of the empty metal click last night when, in despair, he had put the pistol to his temple and pulled the trigger. "I reckon Charley and Lucas thought I wouldn't have no need for 'em out here. When they left, they took everything, even the shells that was already loaded into my gun."

"No bullets at all, huh?" Eddie smiled when he got the idea. "Well, I'll be damned."

Sam stopped when he heard the shot, flat and low in the distance. If he had been closer, he might have thought someone was shooting at him, but it was much too far to be that. Why would they be shooting? Didn't they realize that in so doing, they were giving away their position? Sam reached down to pat the neck of his animal.

"Could be that they know I'm here and they're just lettin' me know they know," Sam suggested to his horse. His horse, almost as if understanding, whickered. Sam chuckled. "That's what you think, too, huh? Well, come on, let's see this thing through."

As Sam moved up the canyon floor he approached carefully by staying close to the wall, taking advantage of the many rocks and protrusions, passing through apertures when possible rather than going around or over the long fingers. When he reached one particularly large protrusion, he saw horse droppings that were just a few hours old. He saw, too, that there were more horse droppings than would be there from the casual passing of an animal. The horse that did this had lingered in this very spot for quite a while.

Sam moved cautiously up to the top of the promontory, then looked over to the other side. He saw a hobbled, saddled horse and Billy Purcell sitting near by, holding a coffee cup and staring into the remains of a fire.

There was something not quite right about the scene, and Sam studied it for a long moment trying to figure out what was wrong. Gradually it began to come to him.

The first thing peculiar was the stillness with which Purcell was sitting there. Sam had been watching him for almost a full minute now, and Purcell had not only not taken a drink of his coffee, he hadn't even moved or twitched. Besides, Sam wondered, if he did have coffee in that cup, where did it come from? There was no pot anywhere, no smell of coffee in the air, and not even a tiny wisp of smoke to indicate that the coals were still warm.

Sam realized then, as much from gut instinct as from what he was seeing, that Purcell was dead. That was what the shot was. They said that the kid who was killed in Salcedo had hit one of the robbers. Sam knew now what happened. Billy Purcell was the one who was hit and, because he was slowing them down, the other two had killed him and left him behind as a decoy.

With a sigh, Sam holstered his pistol and started down into the camp. The carcass was still worth five hundred dollars to him, so there was no way he was going to leave him here. Conveniently Purcell's horse was still here, too, so all Sam would have to do would be throw him belly-down on the saddle and . . . the saddle?

Suddenly Sam realized that something else was wrong! There was one saddle too many! One was on the ground beside the propped-up body of Billy Purcell, and the other was on the horse.

At that moment a rifle cracked and the bullet whistled by, taking off his hat and fluffing his hair. Sam dived to the ground, pulling his pistol from his holster as he did so. He began wriggling on his belly toward a small rock outcropping, reaching it just as a second bullet came so close that he could hear the air pop as it sped by.

When he made it to the rocks, he raised up slowly and looked toward the source of the shot. He didn't see anyone, but he did see a little puff of white smoke drifting slowly to the east. Because the wind was out of the west, that meant that the shooter had to be somewhat west of the smoke. Sam shifted his eyes in that direction, then saw the crown of a hat, rising slowly above the rocks.

Sam waited until he thought enough of the hat was visible to provide a target, then he shot. The hat went sailing away.

"You son of a bitch! You put a hole in my hat!"

"I meant to put a hole in your head," Sam replied. He was puzzled by the voice. This wasn't Charley Harris or Lucas Babbit. Who was it?

The ambusher fired again. The bullet hit the rock right in front of Sam, kicking up tiny pieces of rock and shreds of hot lead to his face before it whined away behind him. Sam turned around and slid down into the ground, brushing the hot lead from his cheeks.

"Did I give you another scar like that purple turd you got layin' across your face now?" the man called.

"Close, but no cigar," Sam replied. "Who the hell are you?"

The man laughed. "You don't recognize me?" he asked. "All I can say is, you sure got yourself one hell of a short memory."

Sam remembered now . . . not the name, but the voice. "You were in the saloon last night," he said. "You were with the two who got themselves killed."

"Yeah. The name's Eddie Webber, in case you forgot."

"Eddie Webber," Sam said. "I'll try to remember that."

"You won't have to remember it too long," Eddie said. He fired again, again coming incredibly close. Sam realized then that Eddie Webber wasn't just another wild cowboy with a gun. He was very good with the rifle.

"I'll say this for you, Eddie Webber. You handle that rifle pretty well."

"Yeah," Eddie said. "There wasn't no way I was goin' to go up against you or the sheriff with a pistol last night. But with a rifle, now, that's a different story. I've won the Fourth-of-July rifle-shooting contest for the last five years running."

"That's pretty good," Sam said.

"Yeah," Eddie replied. "Good enough, I figure, to do me in good stead for my new business."

"Let me guess, Eddie. Would that be the bounty-hunting business?"

"You guessed right," Eddie replied. "I come out here to join up with 'em, only I found Purcell here, all alone. The others had gone on to Aquilla without him. Me and Purcell got to talkin' and the next thing you know, I find out he's worth five hundred dollars. He wasn't lyin' to me, was he Slater? He is worth five hundred dollars?"

"He wasn't lyin'. He's worth that and then some," Sam answered, thinking of the additional reward Judge Smiley had put on his head.

"Yeah, well, five hundred dollars. That's a lot of money," Eddie said. "So I got to thinkin' about it. Why should I join up with these fellas and get a price on my head when I could turn 'em in and get the reward myself? So I killed him."

"Seems like the reasonable thing to do," Sam replied.

During the entire conversation, Sam had been slipping out of his boots, pants, and shirt. Now he put them on the ground behind where he had taken cover, arranging them so that, at a casual glance from a distance, it would look as if he were there. Then, barefoot and half-naked, he put the blade of his knife between his teeth and slipped away. After having gone some thirty yards, he found himself in a narrow, twisting fissure that worked its way down the side of the canyon, passing fairly close to where Eddie had taken cover.

Sam stepped into the fissure and, putting his bare feet and hands on either side, began climbing. Not even a mountain goat would be able to climb up this steep, natural chimney, but Sam wasn't a mountain goat. He was a man who had lived with the Apache . . . a people who could climb where mountain goats could not.

"I figure the first thing I got to do if I'm goin'

to be a success at my new business is get rid of my competition," Eddie said. He chuckled. "That's you, Slater."

Eddie fired again and his bullet nicked the heel of Sam's boot, knocking it back behind the rock.

"Ha!" Eddie shouted. "I'll just reckon that stung a mite, didn't it? That'll learn you to keep your foot out where I can see it."

Sam continued to climb until he reached a ledge. Once there, he left the fissure and crawled out onto it. Then, on his stomach, he wriggled over to the edge and looked down. Eddie was no more than twenty yards below him. Eddie was peering around the side of a rock, looking toward the place where he had last seen Sam.

"Hey, Slater! How come you ain't shootin' back?" Eddie called. "You ain't out of shells, are you? 'Course, if you was, I don't reckon you'd tell me. I mean, Billy Purcell told me an' look what it got 'im. He told me he was out of bullets and I shot him. Like you said, it seemed like the reasonable thing to do."

Eddie fired again.

"If you keep shooting at rocks, you're going to run out of bullets yourself," Sam said easily.

Startled, Eddie turned around. The expression in his face reflected the shock of seeing Sam, not only in a place totally different from where he thought he was, but also because Sam was naked, except for a pair of underbriefs.

"What the hell?" Eddie shouted, swinging his rifle around while, at the same time, jacking in a new round.

Eddie got the lever down, but he never pulled it back up. Sam's right arm whipped forward and the knife flashed once in the sun as it sped across the distance between the two men. It buried itself to the hilt in Eddie's chest, penetrating his heart and killing him even before he could fully realize what was happening to him.

AQUILLA WAS ON THE AMERICAN SIDE OF THE border, but far more Mexicans lived there than Americans. Its primary reason for being was to provide a conduit between Mexico and the United States. Mexican peasants who were leaving their homeland for a better life stopped here on their way north. Americans, many of whom were going to Mexico to escape wanted posters, stopped here on their way south.

The land immediately around Aquilla was arid and too poor for farming or ranching. Many tried, though, and a few even managed to eke out a meager existence. There were some who searched for gold or silver, and though little of those commodities were found, enough nuggets turned up to hold out tantalizing prospects. Thus the hunt continued.

Despite the bleakness of its agricultural and mining industries, Aquilla was a bustling town. It saw a surprising amount of money flow through its half-dozen saloons, whorehouses, gaming establishments, cafés, and hotels. Outlaws fleeing south often used Aquilla for one last American fling. And since many of those same outlaws were fleeing from bank robberies or other sources of ill-gotten gain, money was in abundance. On the other hand, Mexicans just arriving in America would often spend their life savings in one afternoon, too ignorant of the exchange system to know they were being cheated.

Aquilla had a sheriff and two deputies. One wall in the sheriff's office was decorated with wanted posters from both sides of the border. However, neither Sheriff Blakemore nor his deputies had ever made any attempt to apprehend the men on the wanted posters. The way the sheriff explained it, he and his deputies were hired by the people of Aquilla to keep the peace in Aquilla. If a man who had a price on his head in Texas, or Colorado, or Wyoming, or some such place happened to pass through

Aquilla, he was just as welcome as any other traveler, so long as he didn't disturb the peace in Aquilla.

The outlaws were very aware of Sheriff Blakemore's policy toward wanted men, so they were always on their best behavior in his town and around him. In fact, some of them even became friends with him and the sheriff's "rogues' gallery" became somewhat well known throughout the Southwest for a most unique reason. Almost three quarters of the wanted posters on the wall in his office were autographed by the very outlaws whose face graced them.

Babbit was very familiar with Aquilla, having been here many times before. However, it was Charley's first visit, so Babbit explained the ground rules to him as they rode toward the town.

"All you gotta do when we get there is keep your nose clean here," Babbit told him. "Don't get in any fights."

"If nobody messes with me, there won't be no problem," Charley replied.

"No fights, Charley," Babbit repeated. "If somebody messes with you, you're goin' to let them. You understand what I'm saying?"

"This is my gang, Lucas. I give the orders, not you," Charley replied.

Babbit laughed. "Look around, Charley. You been gettin' shed of your gang like a dog scratchin' off fleas. You see anyone left?"

"All right, all right," Charley growled. "I'll stay outta trouble."

"That's a good boy, Charley."

"But I ain't your boy," Charley said, holding up his finger to make his point. "And soon as I can, I'm puttin' together another gang."

"Yeah, Charley, you do that."

"How much longer?" Charley asked. "I'm gettin' hungry for somethin' more'n jerky and thirsty for more'n trail water."

"Couple hours, maybe," Babbit replied. "We'll be there by nightfall."

True to Babbit's estimate, it was just after dark when he and Charley rode into town, butt weary from the long ride down. They had seventy-five dollars apiece from the bank job in Salcedo. In most towns seventy-five dollars would be considered a lot of money, but Babbit was quick to point out that it wouldn't go far here.

"A whore's two dollars anywhere else," he explained. "Here, they're five dollars."

"Mexican or American?" Charley wanted to know.

"Both, I reckon."

Aquilla was dark except for the patches of light that spilled out into the street from the windows and doors of the cantinas. The town was noisy . . . several guitars competed with each other for attention, a few people were singing, and in the back of one of the cantinas, a trumpet ran through several high trills. Laughter and loud voices filled the night air, and occasionally a gunshot would ring out, though the people knew, almost instinctively, that the gunshots were in boisterous fun and nothing more.

"Hey, fellas," a woman called down to them from an upstairs balcony as they rode by. She was leaning over a banister, wearing nothing but an undergarment that was cut low enough to expose the tops of enormous breasts. Her breasts were large because she was large. "Hey, fellas, why don't you come on up here?" she invited. "I'll take both of you on for the price of one."

With her red hair, pasty-white complexion, and flat, twangy accent, she was definitely American.

"You want to give her a try?" Babbit asked.

Charley looked up at the woman, then laughed. "No, I don't think so," he said. He rubbed his crotch. "You know, I think I'll get me a little black-eyed Mexican girl. I like them girls. 'Course, you got to be careful you don't get a Injun. Sometimes it's hard to tell the difference. I got me a woman one time back in Arizona

Territory . . . thought she was Mexican but she turned out to be Injun. You ever had a Injun woman?"

"Yeah," Babbit said.

"How was she?" Charley asked.

"She was Injun," Babbit said without elaboration. He remembered the young Indian girl he and Purdone had raped. All the time he was with her she had just lain there as if she were dead. She didn't even fight him, and that infuriated him so much he started sticking her with a knife, trying to get some reaction from her. When even that didn't get a reaction from her, he got so angry that he killed her, though Purdone protested, saying even a woman who acted dead was better than no woman at all.

Babbit had hacked off the girl's breast and taken it with him. Then, after he got away from Slater in the night shoot-out at the monastery, he scraped the flesh out and dried the skin, intending to make a tobacco pouch. He had never actually used it as a tobacco pouch, though he did carry it with him.

"I've got her tit," he added matter-of-factly.

"You've got what?" Charley asked, surprised by Babbit's comment.

"I've got her tit," Babbit said again. "You want to see it?" He reached down into his pocket, pulled out the dry, leathery bag, and handed it over to Charley.

Charley, thinking it was a joke, took it from him. At first he was sure that it was leather, then he saw a little spongy protrusion and, curious, examined it more closely. Then, suddenly, he realized that the little piece of sponge was actually a nipple. This really was a woman's breast!

"Son of a bitch!" Charley said, handing it back it revulsion. "It really is a tit!"

"I told you it was."

"How can you carry somethin' like that around with you?"

"What are you gettin' so upset about?" Babbit asked. "I told you, it ain't no white woman's tit. It's a Injun woman's tit. Anyhow, where do you get off findin' fault with me? I didn't kill her. Purdone killed her. All I done was hack off her tit. When it comes to killin' women, you're one up on me, what with that doctor's wife you killed."

"I didn't have no choice," Charley replied. "The way she was screamin' she woulda brought half the town in on us. Anyway, what's done is done."

"That's the way I look at it," Babbit said, sticking the grisly souvenir back in his pocket. "What's done is done. What do you say we get us somethin' to drink?"

The drinking establishment was much more Mexican in flavor than American and even had a clacking curtain of beaded strings for its entry rather than the more American bat-wing doors. Inside, the bar was noisy with conversation, half of it in Spanish, half of it in English.

"Hello, señor," a pretty, young Mexican girl said, coming up to Charley. "I am very thirsty and I do not want to drink alone. You will drink with me?"

Charley started to reach for her, then he saw the top of her full, creamy breast, spilling out over her low-cut blouse. He thought of the little piece of leather he had handled just a moment earlier and his blood ran cold. He turned away from her.

"No," he said. "Go find someone else."

"What the hell's the matter with you, Charley?" Babbit asked, surprised by Charley's strange reaction. "I thought you said you wanted some good-lookin' Mexican gal."

"Not . . . not now," Charley said, not wanting to explain to Babbit why he was feeling like he was.

"Well if you don't want her, I do," Babbit said. He put his arm around the girl. "Come on, honey. You want a drink, let's get a whole bottle and go upstairs."

Of the two men, Babbit was clearly the less attractive to the woman. In fact, there was something almost frightening about his yellow eyes and that terrible scar on his face. That was why she had made her initial overture to Charley. But he had refused, and in her business she couldn't afford to be choosy. So she kept the disappointment hidden behind her eyes and pasted on a smile.

"All right," she said to Babbit. "If your friend does not want me, then I will go with you." Teasingly, she put her hand in Babbit's hair and twisted a strand of it around her finger. "If you want me," she added, coquettishly.

"Honey, you come with me and I'll show you just how much I want you," Babbit said, grabbing her and walking over to the bar to buy a bottle.

Charley watched Babbit and the Mexican girl take their bottle up the stairs, then he, too, walked over to the bar.

"Can I get anything to eat here?" he asked.

"Frijoles. Tamales," the bartender answered.

"Anything American?"

"Eggs, señor."

"Steak?"

The bartender nodded. "Sí, steak too."

"Fix me a steak and some eggs," Charley said. "And let me have a pitcher of beer."

"Sí, Señor Charley. Anything you want," the bartender replied.

Charley smiled. "You know who I am? You recognize me?"

"No, señor. But Señor Babbit called you Charley. Is that not your name, señor?"

The smile left Charley's face. "Yeah," he said, somewhat crestfallen. "Yeah, that's my name."

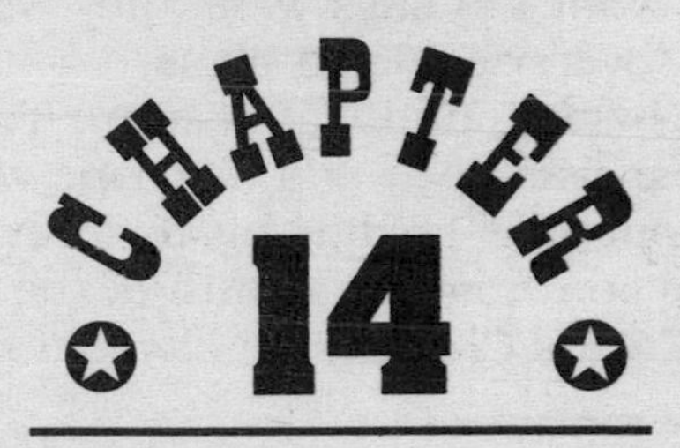

CHARLEY TOOK THE PITCHER OF BEER FROM the bartender and walked over to an empty table in the corner. He sat down with his back to the wall and began drinking his beer. Then he reached into his back pocket and pulled out a rolled-up dime novel and laid it on the table to admire. The pages were torn and the printing was getting dim from sweat, grime, and wear. The drawing on the cover was still discernible, however, and Charley studied it for a long time. It showed a man on a horse, fleeing before a posse. Hanging across the pommel of his saddle were two large bags, and if the reader couldn't figure out what the bags were, they were clearly marked by oversized dollar signs.

In the background was a train. The door of the mail car was open and someone was standing in the opening, holding his fist over his head. A word balloon from the mouth of the character said, *It's Cactus Charley! He has just robbed the express!*

There were several people leaning out the open windows of the cars on the train and all of them seemed to be armed and shooting at the fleeing robber. The robber, who according to the book, was Cactus Charley Harris, was holding the reins of his horse in his teeth while he was twisted around in the saddle, firing both guns at the pursuing posse, two of whom were in the process of falling from their saddles with mortal wounds, inflicted by Cactus Charley's unerring pistol fire.

The cover left unexplained how a posse managed to arrive on the scene so quickly that the train Cactus Charley had just robbed was still sitting on the tracks. It also did not take into account the fact that of all the crimes for which the real Charley Harris was charged, none of them involved robbing a train, which was, in fact, much too dangerous an operation for Charley ever to consider.

The name of the novel was *Cactus Charley's Bold Midnight Robbery of the Denver Express,* though the robbery depicted on the cover was very obviously taking place in daylight.

Charley began to read:

> *He came upon the train with both guns blazing and the reins of his horse held in his teeth. "Stand and deliver!" he shouted in a voice that was both heroic and frightening.*

Charley thought this was a very exciting beginning. He never stopped to wonder how he could even talk with the reins in his teeth, let alone sound off in a voice that was both heroic and frightening. And though he had never used the line *Stand and deliver*, it had a good ring to it and he decided that in his very next holdup he would use it.

> *"It is Cactus Charley," the engineer shouted to his fireman. His voice was laced with fear and respect, for Cactus Charley is known throughout the West as the deadliest shot alive. It has been reliably reported that Cactus Charley can shoot the leg off a fly at fifty paces. There was a shower of sparks and the squeal of steel wheels sliding upon steel rails as the frightened engineer brought his great iron steed to rest.*
>
> *"Open the doors of the express car or feel*

the fury of hot lead!" Cactus Charley demanded.

Though the armed guards of the express car were filled with the greatest of trepidation, the ladies of the train, all of whom had hurried to the windows as a more opportune place from which to get a good look, were strangely devoid of fear. They seemed, instead, romantically smitten by the handsome young man who sat astride his horse, holding the brace of pistols leveled at the express car door.

A plate of steak and eggs was put on the table in front of Charley, but he was too absorbed in the story to bother to look up. He reached for the steak and picked it up in his hands.

"Charley, you really need to work on your table manners," Sam said. "Haven't you ever heard of a knife and fork?"

Gasping, Charley looked up to see that the person who had just delivered his food was not the bartender but Sam Slater. Sam had his pistol out. He waved the end of the barrel.

"Go ahead, take a bite," he said. "I wouldn't want to disturb a man before he was finished eatin' his supper."

Charley held the piece of meat just in front of his mouth, staring wide-eyed at his captor.

"Go ahead, eat," Sam said again.

Charley raised the steak to his mouth, then suddenly dropped it and made a mad grab for his pistol. But Sam was quicker and he brought his pistol down hard on Charley's head. Charley fell like a poleaxed steer.

"You shouldn't read that trash, Charley," Sam said quietly. "You'll get to believing you're better than your are."

Sam bent down to take Charley's pistol. Then he dragged the outlaw's limp, unconscious form over to one of the supporting posts where he propped him and, placing one arm to either side of the post, put the handcuffs on.

The guitar music, laughter, and conversation had all come to a stop when Sam knocked Charley out. Most of the other patrons looked on in curiosity, making no comment until they saw Sam put on the handcuffs.

"Hey, what the hell? You a lawman, mister? 'Cause if you are, you got no jurisdiction here."

Sam looked up at the speaker, then laid a finger alongside his scar. "Who are you?" he asked.

"I'm the man that's goin' to teach you better than to come into Aquilla to serve paper. Who the hell are you?"

"The name is Slater. Sam Slater."

"Slater?" someone said, in a high, choked voice.

"That there is the Regulator," another added in a harsh whisper.

"El Vigilante," one of the Mexicans said in awe.

The man who had challenged Sam began shake. "Don't pay me no mind, mister," he said in a frightened, quavering voice. "You go on about your business."

"Obliged," Sam replied. He walked back over to the table where Charley had been sitting. His untouched steak had fallen back onto his plate and Sam cut off a generous piece of it and stuck it into his mouth. He picked up the pitcher of beer and took several swallows before he sat it back down. The rest of the saloon continued to watch him in silence.

"Play," Sam said to the guitarist.

"Sí, señor," the guitarist said, and he began strumming some chords.

Sam walked over to the bar. "There were two of 'em," he said.

"Sí, señor."

"Where's the other one?"

"Señor, I cannot say," the bartender replied. "Please, do not ask me." Even as he was refusing to speak, however, he flicked his eyes up.

"All right," Sam replied. "I'll find him myself."

Upstairs, in the girl's bedroom, Babbit had heard the saloon below grow strangely quiet. He stopped.

"Are you finished, señor?" the girl asked.

"Shut up," Babbit hissed.

"Qué?" the girl asked, surprised by Babbit's harsh command.

"I said shut up!" Babbit hissed again, putting his hand over her mouth. When he was sure she wouldn't speak again, he pulled his hand away. The girl took a long, gasping breath.

Babbit sat up and swung his legs over the side of the bed, then reached for his pistol. It was still deathly quiet below. "Don't you hear that?" he asked.

"I hear nothing, señor," the girl said in a quiet, whimpering voice.

"Yeah, that's just it," Babbit said. "Neither do I."

Still holding his pistol, he began slipping back into his pants. He was already buttoning them up when the guitar music started again. Even this, however, was different. Before, the music had been soft and melodious, a simple melody weaving in and out of gentle chording. Now it was loud, syncopated, and invasive.

Babbit slipped into his boots and kept his eye on the doorknob. He had just gotten them on when he saw the doorknob move, ever so slightly.

Babbit began firing, punching a pattern of six bullets through the door in such a way that one of them was sure to be fatal to whoever was on the other side.

With an angry shout, Babbit rushed across the room and kicked open the door. He ran out onto the landing just outside the door.

Sam had jiggled the doorknob then stepped to one side, no more than a second before the fusillade of bullets. He stood on one side of the door with his back to the wall, watching the spray of splinters as the bullets came through. Then he heard Babbit's loud, angry shout as the outlaw dashed across the room. When the fugitive appeared on the landing Sam brought his pistol crashing into the back of his head. The blow, plus the momentum of Babbit's rush, carried him through the banister, causing him to crash, belly-down, onto one of the tables in the room below.

By the time Sam reached the bottom of the stairs, Sheriff Blakemore was stepping through the beaded curtains of the front door. He saw all the patrons of the saloon standing to one side or the other, giving Sam a lot of room.

"What the hell is goin' on here?" the sheriff asked.

"I have a couple of prisoners for you,

Sheriff," Sam said. He pointed to Charley. "The one handcuffed to the post is Charley Harris. The other one is Lucas Babbit."

The sheriff shook his head. "I got no call to hold them two fellas," he said. "They ain't done nothin' in my town."

"All I want you to do is keep them overnight while I get a little sleep." Sam reached into his shirt pocket and took out two folded papers. "They're both wanted men," he said. "Here are the dodgers. All I want you to do is keep them overnight. I'll be takin' 'em back with me in the morning."

"They may be wanted men where you come from, mister," the sheriff said. "But like I said, they ain't wanted here. I'm not puttin' 'em in my jail."

By now Charley had come to, and heard the sheriff's refusal to cooperate.

"What are you goin' to do now, Slater?" he asked. "You got to have some rest 'fore you start back. Otherwise you might just drop off to sleep and me or Babbit will get the jump on you." He giggled loudly at his suggestion.

"Don't worry about it, Charley," Sam said. "The sheriff has just changed his mind. He's going to keep you two for me after all."

"Now, just a minute here!" Sheriff Blakemore said. "Where do you come off sayin' a thing like that? I ain't about to change my mind."

Sam's draw was as quick as the flick of a ratler's tongue. He raised his pistol and pointed it at Sheriff Blakemore. "Sheriff, you can go down to the jail house as their jailer or their cell mate. The choice is yours."

"Suppose I don't like either choice?" the sheriff replied.

"There is a third choice," Sam explained. "You can go out of here stretched out flat on your back." He cocked his pistol.

"I'm the sheriff. You wouldn't shoot me."

Sam fired. His bullet clipped off a tiny piece of the sheriff's left earlobe, sending out a spray of blood. The sheriff, with a shout of pain and terror, slapped his hand to his ear. The wound was bleeding profusely and the blood began streaming through his fingers.

"You're . . . you're crazy!" he said.

Sam moved the pistol to aim at the sheriff's other ear. Quickly Blakemore covered it up.

"This time I'll take off a couple of fingers, too," Sam suggested.

"No! No! Wait!" the sheriff said, holding his bloody hands, palms out, toward Sam. "Don't shoot again. I'll put 'em up for you!"

Sam smiled and lowered his gun. "I thank you for your cooperation," he said. "Come first light in the mornin', I'll be by for them."

A CROWING ROOSTER WOKE SAM JUST before first light the next morning. He sat up, stretched, pulled on his boots, then walked over to the chifforobe, where he poured water from a pitcher into a basin and splashed a little onto his face. A few minutes later he tromped downstairs, past the snoring hotel clerk, and out into the early-morning coolness.

Aquilla in the morning and Aquilla in the evening were like two different towns. Last night the streets had been noisy with high-pitched laughter, boisterous song, loud talk, and banging guns, some discharged in fun, some in anger.

But even the most dedicated reveler was in bed now, and the only sounds to be heard were the sounds of the other half of the town . . . the working half . . . coming awake.

A freight wagon was being loaded, and Sam could hear the scrape, roll, and drop of its cargo being put into place.

A woman was doing her wash, and Sam could hear the scruffing sounds of wet clothes being rubbed back and forth across a washboard.

Another early riser was doing some carpentry work and Sam could hear the rip and tear of the saw teeth, chewing into the piece of lumber.

Sam woke the stableboy and paid the fare for his horse and for Charley and Babbit's horses. The animals looked fit and ready for the trip back to Gunther. That was good, since he had no desire to have his trip interrupted by problems with one of the mounts.

Sam rode his horse and led the other two down to the far end of the street. It was curious, he thought, how three horses could walk down a main street at high noon and barely be heard. This morning, however, the fall of their hooves seemed so loud that he doubted if he could have made any more noise had he been banging on a drum. He stopped in front of the sheriff's office and tied up at the hitching rail.

The sheriff was already up this morning, sitting at his desk. He had a bandage covering his shot-up ear; it was wound all the way around his head. As a result he looked much more seriously hurt than he was. He was drinking coffee and eating a biscuit and he glared at Sam when Sam came into the office.

"Good morning, Sheriff," Sam said. "Good, you fixed breakfast."

"Not for you I didn't," the sheriff growled.

Sam walked over to the stove and hefted the coffeepot, then he opened the saver and looked it to see a pan full of biscuits.

"That's for my deputies," the sheriff said.

Sam clinked a half-dollar down on the corner of the sheriff's desk. "Tell 'em to get their breakfast somewhere else," he ordered. He filled two cups, then grabbed four biscuits and started back to the cells. "Charley, Babbit, wake up," he called. "It's time to be goin'." He passed the coffee and biscuits through the bars.

"You poison this?" Charley asked.

"Now, why would I poison you, Charley?" Sam answered good-naturedly. "If I didn't want to see you hang, I would've shot you last night. Besides, seein' as how you missed your supper, I figured you might be hungry this morning."

Babbit took his breakfast without comment,

and the two men returned to their bunk where they sat down to eat.

"Don't get to thinking you're having breakfast at Delmonico's," Sam told them. "Swallow that down pretty quick. I'm about to have a little breakfast of my own, and when I'm done, we're leavin', whether you're finished or not."

As Sam ate his biscuit and drank his coffee, he studied Sheriff Blakemore's rogues' gallery, aware that the sheriff was still glaring at him from behind. After a moment or two Sam turned toward the sheriff.

"I don't reckon it matters none to you that half a dozen or more of these fellas are dead already," he said.

"You kill 'em?"

"Some of them," Sam said.

"How does it feel, Slater, makin' a livin' by killin' folk?"

"I don't kill for a living, Sheriff," Sam replied evenly. "When I can, I take them in. If I'm forced to kill someone, it's his choice. And I can live with that a lot better than I could live with being a sheriff who has sworn to protect the public but who has sold out to the outlaws."

"I haven't sold out to anybody," Blakemore said resolutely. He pointed to his rogues' gallery. You think any of those men have given me money not to arrest them?"

"It doesn't matter whether you've taken any

money from them or not. You've sold out to them just to buy a little peace in your town." Sam turned up his cup and swallowed the last of his coffee. "But that's your problem, not mine," he said. He set his empty cup on the sheriff's desk. "I'll get these two out of your hair."

Sam walked over to the wall hook and took down the key ring.

"Slater?" Blakemore called. Sam stopped and looked toward the sheriff. Blakemore ran his hand through his hair, then adjusted the bandage around his head. "Watch out on the trail," he said. "I heard some talk."

"What sort of talk?"

"A few of the boys got together last night," he said. "They figure if they can kill you and free your two prisoners, it'll be a sign to all the other bounty hunters and lawmen that Aquilla should be left alone."

"Thanks for the warning," Sam said.

"Yeah. Well, I'll be honest with you. If they get the job done, I ain't goin' to lose no sleep over it," Blakemore said. "But bushwhackin' a man on the trail . . . that's goin' too far, even for me."

"Do you have any idea where this is supposed to happen?"

"No," Blakemore said. "I told you all I know. The rest is up to you."

* * *

Sam rode behind Charley and Babbit, using his proven method of securing them to each other and to him by hangman's nooses. To be honest, he wasn't one-hundred-percent certain that the nooses would really break their necks if they attempted to run. This was because the fear the nooses instilled in his prisoners was great enough that no one had ever tried it.

They crossed a little stream and Sam watched the hooves kick up silver sprays of water as they went across.

"Hey," Babbit called. "Let's stop here for water."

"We've got enough water in our canteens," Sam said.

"The water in our canteens tastes like piss," Babbit said. "This will be good cold water."

Babbit was right. The stream was swiftly running and cool and it would be good. And the water in their canteens was tepid and sour. But if they stopped here, it might well be Sam's last stop. That was because for some time now Sam had been aware that three men were dogging them, riding parallel with them and for the most part staying out of sight. This would be a perfect spot for them to try their ambush if they were going to. Sam didn't plan to give them that opportunity.

"I think my horse is going lame," Charley said a short while later.

"Do you?"

"Yeah, can't you see him. He's favorin' his left foreleg somethin' awful."

"Not that I can see," Sam said.

"Well, then, you're blind," Charley said. "We've got to stop. We've got to stop, I tell you, and give him a rest. Maybe he's just picked up a stone or something."

Since both men had tried to make him stop, Sam knew then that they were aware that an ambush was being planned. They were doing all in their power to give the bushwhackers every opportunity to be successful.

Sam looked over to his left without being obvious about it and saw three riders slipping through a notch in the hills, moving so quietly and expertly that only someone who was specifically looking for them would have noticed.

Ahead of them was a narrow draw. While they were in the draw they would be protected, but when they emerged from the other end, they would for a while be totally exposed, while any would-be ambushers would have the cover of an outcropping of rocks. Sam knew that the ambush would take place at this place, but he had no idea what he was going to do to thwart it.

Then, as soon as they entered the draw, Sam ordered them to stop.

"Stop? What for?" Charley replied.

"You said you were afraid your horse was going lame. Here's your chance to take a look at him," Sam suggested.

"Yeah, well, now I don't think it was anything," Charley replied. "I think he just picked up a small stone, then threw it, that's all. He's doin' fine now."

"Stop anyway," Sam said, giving a small jerk on the rope.

"All right, all right!" Charley complained. "Be careful with that rope. You're goin' to break our necks if you don't watch out."

"No," Sam said. "I'm goin' to break your neck if *you* don't watch out. Now climb down."

The two prisoners climbed down. Charley started to go through the motions of looking at his horse's hoof.

"Don't bother with that," Sam said.

"What?"

"There's nothing wrong with your horse. You know it and I know it."

"Then why did we stop?"

"Because I want to change shirts and hats with you."

"What? Why would you want to do that?"

"Because I like your shirt better."

"You're crazy," Charley said. He started to

get back onto his horse, but he was stopped when he heard the metallic click of Sam's pistol being cocked.

"Maybe you didn't hear me. I said take off your shirt and hat," Sam repeated.

"Now that just don't make no sense at all. And anyhow I can't. My hands are cuffed."

Sam held up the key and motioned Charley toward him. Puzzled by Sam's strange request, Charley moved toward him, holding out his hands. Sam released the handcuffs, then Sam, and then Charley, began taking off their shirts.

"What about me?" Babbit said. "Don't I get to get naked, too?"

"Your turn will come," Sam said.

"My turn will come? My turn will come for what? What the hell has got into you?" Babbit asked.

"Don't worry about it," Sam said. "I'll tell you what you need to know when you need to know it."

A moment later Charley had put on Sam's shirt and started to get back on his horse.

"No," Sam said. "Ride this horse for a while."

"Would you mind tellin' me just what the hell you are doin'?" Charley asked.

"Mount up," Sam said. "You ride back there, I'll ride up here with Babbit."

"This don't make no sense," Charley mumbled as he mounted Sam's horse.

Remounted, the men rode through the long, narrow draw toward the bright wedge of light at the far end. The horses' hooves clattered loudly against the stone and the echoes tumbling back to them made it sound as if an entire troop of men were riding through instead of only three.

It wasn't until the three horses emerged at the other end that Charley suddenly figured out what Sam was doing.

"No!" he shouted out loud. "No, don't shoot! Don't shoot!"

"Charley, what the hell's got into you?" Babbit hissed.

"Don't you see what this son of bitch has done?" Charley shouted. "He's got me wearin' his duds an' ridin' his horse! Bates! Carlisle! McGreggor! Don't shoot! It's me, Charley!"

One of the three bushwhackers stood up about one hundred yards up the trail. He could be seen from the waist up, but only in silhouette against the bright sky.

"All right, Slater," the bushwacker called. "You pulled a pretty good one on us this time. But you got a long way to go, and I don't think you're goin' to get there."

The silhouette disappeared, and, a moment later, Sam heard the clatter of horses being ridden at a gallop.

"You think you're so goddamned smart," Charley said. "They'll just find someplace else.

And this time they won't be fooled by changing shirts and horses."

"Charley," Sam said, giving the rope one more good tug. Charley let out a choking sound. "You talk too damned much."

MCGREGGOR LAY ON THE TOP OF THE FLAT rock, looking back along the trail over which they had just come. He saw the three riders moving slowly but steadily to the north. From this distance he had no idea which one of the three might be Slater, but it didn't matter. Even if he did know, he was much too far out of range to do anything about it.

Behind him, Bates and Carlisle sat resting. Bates was chewing on the root of a grass stem. Carlisle had his boot off, examining a blister.

"You see 'em?" Bates asked.

"Yeah. They're 'bout a mile behind us."

"You figured out who is who yet?"

"No," McGreggor admitted. "Even if I did, there ain't noplace we could set up a ambush between there and here. And I sure as hell don't plan to go out into the open to take him on."

"Why not? There's five of us and only one of him."

"Where do you get five?" Carlisle asked. It was the first time he had spoken, as he had been too interested in the blister on his toe.

"Well, you gotta count Babbit and Charley Harris as bein' on our side," Bates said.

"Why? What the hell can they do? They ain't even armed."

"Well, I don't know. They can do somethin'," Bates suggested. "Get in the way so he can't get off a shot, or somethin'."

"They'll get in the way, all right. They'll get themselves killed and us, too," Carlisle said. "If we get another chance at an ambush like before, I say we ought to do it."

"I know the country from here to Gunther," McGreggor said. "We won't get another chance like the one we just had."

"Yeah? Well, maybe there is another place," Bates suggested.

"Where?" Carlisle asked as, wincing in pain, he put his boots back on. "'Cause what I'd like to do is kill this son of a bitch and get it over with."

"There ain't no way he's goin' to get back to Gunther without goin' through Three Wells, and there ain't no way he's going through there without stoppin' for the night. We'll be waitin' for him there."

"Yeah," Carlisle said, smiling broadly. "Yeah, that's a good idea. And maybe we can have a few drinks while we wait."

To prevent any ambush on the trail Sam had Charley and Babbit change shirts and hats a couple more times so that anyone watching from a distance would be thoroughly confused as to who was who. By the time they approached Three Wells, however, they were back in their proper attire.

As they rode by boot hill they saw four fresh graves. One of them was the grave of Billy Purcell.

"I see you killed poor Billy," Charley said.

Sam shook his head. "No," he said. "Eddie Webber shot him, but you're the one killed him, Charley. All I'm doing is collecting the reward."

"You're a coldhearted son of a bitch, you know that?" Charley said. "I mean, to take advantage of another man's misery like that."

"The reward was there, the body was there," Sam said. "If I don't collect on it, someone else will."

As the three men rode toward the jail, the fact that two of them were connected by noosed rope caught the attention of many of the townspeople.

"Hey! It's Sam Slater!" someone called.

"Slater's back, and he has Harris and Babbit with him!"

"I knew them boys wouldn't get away from the Regulator!"

As the shouted news traveled from one to another, a crowd began to build and the crowd followed the horsemen down the street, running along on the boardwalk, or hurrying through the dirt. Several young boys, using bent twigs as toy guns, shot at each other as they hurried along side.

"Bang, bang! I'm the Regulator and you're Charley Harris and you're dead! Bang, bang!"

"No! I'm the Regulator and you're Charley Harris!"

"I don't want to be Charley Harris. Charley Harris is going to hang."

"So's Lucas Babbit!"

"Wish they'd do it here so we could watch, don't you?"

Charley, who couldn't help but overhear the shouted argument, stared straight ahead and licked his lips nervously.

Slater chuckled. "What's the matter, Charley? You're looking a little peaked."

"Those kids," Charley growled. "Somebody ought to teach them manners."

By the time they reached the jail, Sheriff Pratt was standing on the front porch, smiling. "Well, Slater, came back to pay us another visit, I see."

"Can you keep these two for me overnight?" Sam asked, swinging down from his horse.

"Be glad to," Pratt said. "Come on, you two, we got a nice quiet cell just waitin' for you."

"Have 'em ready to go by sunup, would you, Sheriff?"

"They'll be ready. Why don't you head on down to the saloon? Dr. Shelby, Mitch, Marcus, Andy, and the others are plannin' on givin' you all you can eat and drink, I think."

"Thanks," Sam said. "Maybe I'll just do that."

When Sam stepped into the saloon a few minutes later, Belle was actually the first one to greet him. She slid her arm through his and escorted him over to the same table where he had played cards with Doc and the others a few days earlier. A pitcher of beer and a clean glass was already there, and no sooner had he sat down than someone brought him a plate of beans.

"We got you a steak cookin', too, if you want it," Mitch said.

"Steak sounds good," Sam admitted. He picked up the fork. "And the beans smell good," he added, taking a bite.

In the far corner of the same saloon, Bates, Carlisle, and McGreggor sat nursing a whiskey.

"Look at the way they gather around him," McGreggor said. "You'd think the son of a bitch was just like Abraham Lincoln or somebody."

"Maybe he is," Bates suggested.

"What are you talkin' about, maybe he is?"

Bates looked at the other two and smiled. "Well, as I recollect, Lincoln got shot, didn't he?"

McGreggor and Carlisle laughed out loud.

"Yeah," Carlisle said. "Yeah, he did at that."

"Let's drink a toast to old Abe," Bates offered, and laughing, the other two held their glasses out and joined in the toast.

Sam ate and drank his fill that evening, though he begged out of a repeat of the card game with the excuse that he was tired and had a lot of distance to cover the next day. "I'm going to get the biggest bed in the quietest room in the hotel," he told the others. "And I'm going to sleep the sleep of the dead."

"D'ya hear that?" Bates hissed. "The son of a bitch wants to sleep the sleep of the dead."

"Well, we'll just have to see if we can help him out," Carlisle replied.

Sam waved good-bye to his well-wishers in the saloon, then walked over to the hotel. He asked for, and got, the room overlooking the street.

"Will you require a knock on your door to

awaken you, Mr. Slater?" the desk clerk asked.

"I'll probably wake myself," Slater said as he signed the guest registration book. "But if you haven't seen me by sunup, give me a yell."

"Yes, sir, Mr. Slater. It'll be my pleasure."

Sam climbed the stairs then started down the long corridor toward his room. The corridor was well lighted with wall-mounted gas lanterns, which heated and filled the hallway with their quiet hissing sound. Once Sam was in his room and with the door closed behind him, it was dark, cool, and inviting. The window was open and a gentle night breeze lifted the gauze curtains.

Sam lit the lantern alongside his bed, took his gun belt off, then stepped up to the open window and looked out onto the dark street below. From here he could see the side of the jail and the small barred window of the cell where Sheriff Pratt had put his prisoners. He saw no one, but it was dark inside the cell, so even if someone was standing at the window, he wouldn't have been able to see them. He yawned and stretched, then went over to extinguish the lamp and plunge his room into darkness.

"There!" Bates said. "Did you see the son of a bitch standing there in his window, just as cool as you please?"

"Yeah, I saw him," Carlisle said. "You'd think he'd have better sense than to stand there like that. Why, if we'da had a rifle, we coulda picked him off like shootin' a fish in a barrel."

"And if a frog had wings, he wouldn't bump his ass ever' time he jumps," Bates growled. "Come on, let's go down to the jail and have a word with Charley and Babbit."

The three men walked back to the rear of the saloon, then moved along behind the row of buildings toward the jail. They were assailed by unpleasant odors, from stale beer, to privies, to garbage dumps of rotted food, though they were odors of such familiarity that the men scarcely noticed.

"There it is," Bates said, when they reached the rear of the barbershop.

The three men moved quickly across the narrow space between the barbershop and the jail, then stood up against the wall of the jail. Here the shadows and darkness shielded them from view, even if someone had been walking down the street right in front of the jail.

"Hey!" McGreggor called. "Hey, Babbit! Charley! You in there?"

Babbit's face appeared in the window of the cell. "Yeah, we're here," Babbit said. "Where've you guys been? We haven't seen you since early this mornin'."

"I know. After Slater pulled that trick on us,

we didn't get another chance," McGreggor said. "Until now."

"Now? What are you goin' to do now?" Charley asked, his face joining Babbit's in the cell window.

"Slater's took him a room over to the hotel," McGreggor explained. "Soon's we're sure he's asleep good, we're goin' to go over and take care of him, once and for all."

"Forget about him," Charley said. "Get us out of here."

"Not yet."

"What do you mean not yet, you bastards?" Charley hissed. "Goddammit, Slater's plannin' on takin' us back to hang! Get us out of here!"

"If we get you out before we get Slater, he'll just come after us all," McGreggor said. "And I don't want that son of a bitch on my tail."

"He's right, Charley," Babbit said. "Slater's like a bulldog. Once he gets hold of you, he don't let go. I know that better'n anybody."

"Well, get us out of here and we'll help you get him," Charley suggested.

"Huh-uh," McGreggor replied, shaking his head. "Me an' Bates an' Carlisle done talked it over. If we get you out now, Slater's liable to hear the commotion and we'll lose our chance at him. I'm tellin' you, right now is the best chance there's ever been to kill him."

"Yeah," Bates added. "And think what all we

can do once Slater is dead. Hell, we can prob'ly get a reward from just about ever'one that's on the dodge."

"All right, all right," Charley agreed reluctantly. "Kill the son of a bitch. I want him dead just as much as anyone . . . prob'ly more'n most people. But don't leave us to rot here once you get the job done."

"Don't worry, you won't be rottin' here. Once we get the job done, this town will be ours," McGreggor promised.

"When you goin' to do it?"

"'Bout midnight. Right now we're goin' to go back and have a few drinks to wile away the time. Then, 'bout midnight, we'll mosey on over to the hotel and do the job."

"Listen for the shots," Carlisle added. "When you hear the shots, you'll know it's us, takin' care of business."

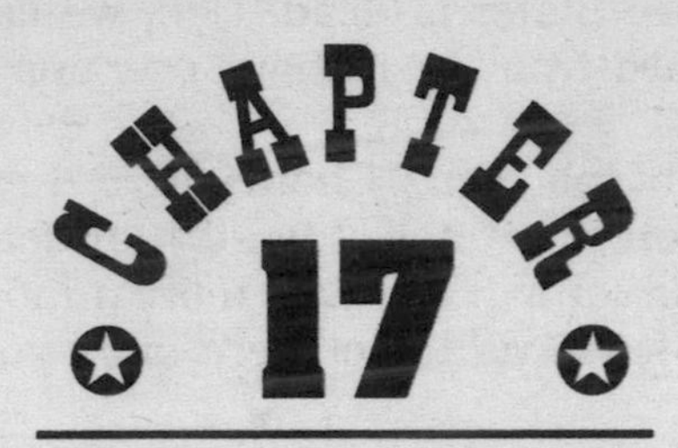

THE GIRL GOT UP FROM THE BED AND WALKED over to the chifforobe, where she poured water into the large porcelain basin. When she saw Carlisle staring at her, she picked up the basin and went behind the dressing screen.

"What the hell did you do that for?" Carlisle asked.

"There are some things a girl needs to do in private," she answered. There was a ripple of water as she dipped the washcloth into the basin.

"You ain't a girl, you're a whore," Carlisle said gruffly. "And since I paid for your time, there ain't none of it private. Now take down that there screen."

There was another rippling sound of water, but the screen stayed up.

"I said, take down that there screen!" Carlisle shouted, and he got out of bed and knocked the dressing screen across the room. It hit the wall, then splintered.

The girl let out a quick shout of fear, then cringed, frightened that he was about to hit her.

"I ain't goin' to hit you," he said. "I'm just goin' to watch. Now go on about your business."

The girl, sobbing silently in fear and embarrassment, dipped the cloth in the water and continued her ablutions. There was a loud knock on the door.

"Belle! Belle, you all right?" a man's voice called.

"Don't you worry none about the little girlie," Carlisle called back. "She's just fine."

"Belle?" the voice called again.

"Go on about your business," Carlisle said. "I told you the girl is just fine."

"I want to hear her voice," the man outside the door insisted.

Carlisle walked over to his pants and pulled his pistol from his holster. He pointed it at the door and cocked it.

"I ain't a-goin' to tell you no more," he said.

"No, don't!" Belle shouted. "Smokey, it's all right! I'm fine."

"You sure? I thought I heard you yell," Smokey's voice called from the other side of the door.

"It's all right, really," Belle said. "I . . . I knocked over the dressing screen by accident, that's all."

"All right," Smokey said reluctantly. "But you call me if you need me."

"Go on back to your drinkin', cowboy," Carlisle said. "And let us get back to our business." He laughed mockingly.

"I'll . . . I'll be downstairs," Smokey said.

Belle stood up.

"What are you doin'?" Carlisle asked.

"I'm finished," she said.

"You're finished? That's all there is to it?"

Belle nodded.

"Hell, what was you so private about? You didn't do nothin' but splash a little water onto yourself."

"Do you want me to bathe you?" she asked.

"What?" Carlisle asked, covering himself indignantly. "No! I took me a bath not no more than a few days ago. I done it all by myself. And if and when I need another'n, why, I'll take that one by myself, too. Fact is, why'n't you just turn your back now an' let me get dressed?"

"Whatever you say," Belle said, waiting until

she turned before she smiled at his sudden case of modesty.

Carlisle was still packing his shirttail down in his pants as he came down the stairs to join Bates and MeGreggor.

"How was she?" McGreggor asked.

"You want to know how she was, you spend your own money," Carlisle said.

"Don't need to," McGreggor said. "I figure you'll pay for it, then you won't be able to keep quiet about it. Pretty soon you'll be talkin' about it so much we won't be able to get you to shut up."

"You don't say," Carlisle replied. "Well, I ain't talkin' yet. What time is it?" he asked.

Bates pointed to the clock on the wall behind the bar. "Accordin' to that, it's near on to midnight," he said.

"You think he's asleep yet?"

"I reckon he is. He had a hard day and he figures to get up early for another hard day tomorrow. I reckon he's asleep by now."

Carlisle smiled, then loosed the pistol in his holster. "Then, what do you say we pay the son of a bitch a visit?"

Carlisle, Bates, and McGreggor left the saloon, then slipped quickly and quietly through the dark of night to the front of the hotel. There, they stopped.

"Look around!" Bates hissed. "You see the sheriff or one of his deputies makin' rounds?"

"I don't see nobody," McGreggor replied.

"All right, let's go in."

The lobby was lighted by only one small lamp, so it was fairly dark. It was deserted as well, for the scattering of chairs and sofas that were sometimes occupied by guests were all empty. Only the night clerk was in the lobby and he was sitting in a chair behind the desk. His chair was tipped back and his head was slumped forward. His chest was rising and falling in rhythm with his snores.

"Get your guns out, gents, and be quiet," Bates whispered, pulling his own pistol.

With guns drawn, they slipped through the shadows of the lobby, then started up the stairs. When they reached the landing, Bates held his finger to his lips. Here, the light was so bright they had to squint.

"Get those damned lights out!" Bates ordered, and McGreggor moved quickly down the corridor, extinguishing each lamp until the hallway was a long tunnel of darkness.

"Come on!" McGreggor hissed loudly. "That's his door down there!"

The three men moved silently through the dark hall until they were just outside the door.

"Shall we break it in?" Carlisle asked.

"I don't know," Bates replied. "If we don't get

it the first time, he'll hear the commotion and we'll be sittin' ducks out here."

"How else we goin' to get in?" Carlisle wanted to know.

"Why don't we just try the doorknob?" McGreggor suggested, turning it slowly.

"You stupid or somethin'? You think he'd be crazy enough to leave it unlocked?" Carlisle asked.

The door swung open.

"Would you look at that? He didn't even lock it," Bates said, voicing the surprise of all of them.

"Go on in."

The room was slightly brighter than the hallway, because of the pale moonlight that fell in through the open window. They could see the bed and Slater's hat and pistol belt, hanging from the brass bedpost.

"This is goin' to be like takin' candy from a baby," Bates said, aiming at the bed.

Bates fired and his shot was followed almost immediately by the other two, so that, for a moment, all three guns were firing, lighting up the darkness with white flashes and filling the room with thunder.

After they had fired three shots apiece, Bates shouted to stop firing. "The whole town will be in here in a minute. We got to get out of here," he said. "Check and make sure the son of a bitch is dead!"

McGreggor walked over to the bed and felt around, then gasped in surprise. "Bates! He ain't here!" he shouted.

"What? Where is he?"

"I'm right here," Sam said. He was standing on the porch roof, just outside his window.

With shouts of frustrated rage and fear, all three would-be assassins turned their guns toward the window and began firing. Bullets crashed through the window, sending large shards of glass out onto the porch roof. Sam had jumped to one side of the window as soon as he spoke, so he avoided the initial fusillade. After the first volley he leaned around and fired into the room. He hit one of the men and saw him go down. The other two bolted through the door.

At first Sam planned to go after them by climbing back into the room, but he knew they would be leaving the hotel, so he decided to just wait until they were on the street. There, they would have fewer places to hide . . . and there would be less likelihood of an innocent bystander being hurt.

Sam, who had been sleeping on the porch roof, fully clothed, ran to the edge of the roof, then jumped down into the space between the hotel and the building next door. He waited there in the shadows and kept his eyes on the front door of the hotel. As he expected, the door burst open a moment later and two men ran out. Sam stepped out into the street to brace them.

"Hold it right there!" he called to them.

"It's Slater!" one of the two men shouted, and he fired.

The bullet whizzed by Sam's ear, much closer than was comfortable, and Sam returned fire, shooting above and just to the right of the shooter's flame pattern. He heard a grunt of pain.

The lone survivor darted across the street and disappeared into the darkness on the other side.

Crouching low, Sam moved back into the darkness on his side of the street, then began searching, trying to find his quarry. A door opened from somewhere behind him, and one of the townspeople came out, carrying a rifle. It was Dr. Shelby."

"What's goin' on? Did Babbit and Charley Harris escape?"

"No," Sam said. "But a few of their friends are tryin' to get 'em out."

The assailant fired from the shadows on the other side of the street and his bullet hit the post between Sam and Doc, sending pieces of wooden splinters into their faces.

"Damn, that hurt!" Doc said.

"Get back in the shadows, Doc," Sam said. "No sense in you gettin' hurt."

"I just want to help."

"You won't be helpin' anyone by gettin' yourself killed."

Suddenly a horse burst out of the shadows from across the street, and its rider, bending low, began firing toward Sam.

Sam shot back, missing the rider, but hitting a lit kerosene lantern than hung on a piece of wood sticking out over the street from the corner of the leather-goods store. Sam's bullet burst the kerosene tank and sent the fuel up into the lighted chimney, causing the lantern to explode. When it did so, it sent a shower of flaming kerosene onto the rider's back.

"Ahhhhiieee!" the rider screamed in terror and pain as he galloped down the street, flaming now like a human torch.

Sam reached for Doc's rifle, jacked a round into the chamber, then raised it to his shoulder. He took a long, careful aim at the ball of fire that had now panicked his horse into galloping faster than ever. By now the outlaw was at the far end of the street, better than two hundred yards away.

Sam squeezed the trigger and the rifle fired, then kicked back against his shoulder. At the far end of the street the fleeing, flaming, rider pitched out of his saddle with a bullet in the back of his head, dead before he ever hit the dirt. He lay there on the ground, burning for several seconds, until a couple of the citizens from that end of town, having been awakened by the commotion, hurried out into the street to douse the flames.

By now Sheriff Pratt was on the scene, wearing pants, boots, and his undershirt. He hadn't even bothered to strap on his pistol, though he was carrying a rifle.

"What happened?" he asked.

"Some men tried to bushwhack Slater, here," Doc explained.

"Locals?" the sheriff asked in surprise.

Sam shook his head. "They were from Aquilla," he explained. "They tried earlier today. I thought they might try again tonight, so I was ready for them." He pointed to the body lying nearby in the street, already drawing a crowd of curious onlookers. "There's one there," he said. "There's another up in my room, and that one down there."

Sheriff Pratt shook his head and chuckled. "Ready for them, huh? I guess you were."

THREE WELLS HAD TELEGRAPHED AHEAD the news that Sam Slater would be arriving with Charley Harris and Lucas Babbit, so when the three men rode into Gunther, the entire town had turned out to meet them.

"Did they give you much of a fight, Slater?" someone called.

"Hey, Cactus Charley, you think you'll get away this time?"

"I'll be comin' to your dance, Charley!"

Charley stared ahead glumly, and when they reached the jail, Sheriff McQuade and Judge Smiley were standing there on the porch to meet them.

"Well, Charley, welcome home," Sheriff McQuade said.

"You go to hell," Charley snarled.

"Now, that's no way to be," McQuade said.

"I hope you got somethin' to eat in there," Charley said. "That son of a bitch ain't fed us nothin' but jerky for three days." Charley started toward the front door of the jail house, but Sheriff McQuade reached out his hand to stop him.

"Huh-uh, Charley, you won't be goin' in there," he said.

"What do you mean?"

"Boys, take him over to the courtyard and put him in the holding cell."

"The holding cell?" Charley said in dread. "No! What are you goin' to put me there for?"

"Why, Charley, don't you remember?" McQuade said. "That's where you were headed when you escaped."

"Yeah, but you don't go there until just before you hang. What is this, a lynchin'? Don't I even get a trial first?"

"You've had your trial," Judge Smiley replied. "There's no need to try you again. You were found guilty, you were sentenced to hang, and hang you shall, this very afternoon."

"Babbit, do somethin'," Charley said as a couple of deputies led him toward the courthouse. "They're fixin' to hang me!"

"Charley, boy, if I was you, I wouldn't be worryin' none 'bout the hanging," Babbit said. "I'd be worryin' 'bout what you're goin' to say to Ray Barnett, and Kelly Sims, and Billy Purcell when you run into 'em down in hell. You know, you just left them boys to die, and I don't reckon they're goin' to treat you too kindly when they see you again."

"You . . . you left 'em, too," Charley said.

"Maybe so, but they wasn't my gang, they was yours," Babbit replied. "Besides which, I ain't goin' to hang this afternoon. You are."

"You son of a bitch! I'll see you in hell!" Charley shouted as they took him away.

Babbit began to laugh.

"I don't know what you have to laugh about, mister," Sheriff McQuade said. "I figure we'll have you tried tomorrow mornin' and hung by tomorrow afternoon."

"Yeah? Well, I ain't got no rope around my neck yet. And you can ask the Regulator here, I ain't that easy to hold on to. Tell him, Slater. Tell him!" Babbit said, with a mocking laugh.

"Babbit, most of the time I turn you people in, collect the money, then leave. But this time I'm going to stay around to watch you hang. And if the sheriff's arm is sore, I might even pull the handle myself."

"I'll have the money ready for you this afternoon," Judge Smiley said.

"Soon enough," Sam replied. "I'd like to take a bath, get a good, hot meal, then a hotel room. If I'm goin' to wait around to see Babbit hang, I'm going to wait in comfort."

"You son of a bitch! You'll never see me hang!" Babbit said.

"Get him inside," Judge Smiley ordered and Sheriff McQuade and the remaining deputy escorted Babbit into the jail.

By two o'clock in the afternoon, Sam had bathed, put on a clean shirt and pants, and was in Judge Smiley's office for his money.

"I've got it right here for you," Judge Smiley said, taking it out of his desk drawer. "The reward I promised you for Harris, plus the reward that was already posted for Sims and Purcell. And I must tell you, I have never paid out a reward with more pleasure. That is one bunch of men I am glad to see gone." He counted out the money, then handed it to Sam.

"Thanks," Sam said. "What time will Babbit's trial be tomorrow?"

"Nine in the morning," Judge Smiley said. "We'll hang him at two."

"I'll be here."

Judge Smiley stroked his chin. "You know, you got paid quite a bit more for Charley Harris and his bunch than you did for Babbit. Yet I get the distinct feeling you got more satisfaction from bringing him in than all the others put together."

"I did."

"Why?"

"I saw the girl," Sam said.

"The girl? Oh, yes, you mean the Indian girl he mutilated. Yes, I suppose that was a grisly scene."

"I knew her," Sam added.

"I see. Then that would make it worse. Well, Mr. Slater, I not only congratulate you, I commend you for not letting your personal feelings get in the way of doing your job. I know you were tempted to kill Babbit yourself, and under the circumstances, if you had done it, you would probably have gotten away with it. I admire your respect for the law."

Sam smiled dryly. "Respect for the law has nothing to do with it," he said. "I never met anyone yet who wouldn't rather be shot than hung."

There was a knock on the door and Judge Smiley yelled for whoever it was to come in. It was his law clerk.

"Judge," the clerk said. "They got Charley Harris standin' on the gallows. The sheriff is waitin' for your signal."

"Yes," Judge Smiley said. He sighed and looked up at Sam. "You know, Mr. Slater, I can sentence someone to die . . . and in the case of a person like Charley Harris . . . a cold-blooded murderer, I can do it with a clear conscience. But when it comes to the part where I actually have to give the signal to dispatch the soul of another human being into eternity . . . I must confess to having qualms." He walked over to the window. "Come, watch with me," he said. "After all, you have a hand in this, too."

Sam walked over to the window and looked down into the courtyard. Three or four hundred people had gathered around the gallows. There were reporters and a photographer in the front row, though since Charley had just been brought in that same morning, the reporters were local only, there being insufficient time to gather any from the national newspapers.

Charley was standing just under the cross beam with the noose around his neck and a hood over his face. His hands were manacled to his belt, so that his arms were stiffly by his sides. His legs were tied together. Any last words he may have had were already spoken at this point, and he was quietly counting off the last seconds of his life.

Judge Smiley nodded his head, and down on the gallows, Sheriff McQuade, who had been awaiting the signal, pulled the handle. From his position at the open window in Judge Smiley's office, Sam could hear the thump of the dropping trapdoor, then the oohs and aahs of the assembled crowd. Charley Harris dropped straight and true, turned one half turn to the left, then was very still.

Though the sun was a full disk up in the east, Sam was still sound asleep when he was awakened by a loud banging on his hotel room door. He sat up quickly, drawing his gun from the holster that hung on the bedstead.

"What is it?" he shouted gruffly.

"Slater, it's me, Sheriff McQuade. Open up."

Still holding his gun, Sam walked over to the door and opened it slightly, just to make certain the sheriff was alone. When he saw that he was alone, he opened it all the way.

"Yeah, come on in," he invited. He took his pants off the back of the chair and started putting them on. As he did so he saw the look of agitation on the sheriff's face. "Babbit?" he asked.

"Yes. How did you know?"

"Just a hunch."

"When I came to the office this morning, I found my night deputy lying dead, just outside the cell. His throat had been cut. Evidently Babbit lured him over to the cell on some pretext, then managed to cut his throat and get the keys."

"You seem to have a hell of a time holding on to your prisoners, Sheriff," Sam said.

"I . . . I can't deny that," McQuade said. "I don't know where he got the knife. We searched him thoroughly before we put him in the cell."

"Babbit is a pretty resourceful man," Sam said. "He probably made the knife out of something he found in the cell."

"Maybe so. Well, he's well armed and well mounted. He took a pistol and holster from the office."

Sam pulled on his boots, then strapped on his gun. "So am I," he said.

"Then you're going after him? You'll bring him back?"

"You asked two questions, Sheriff," Sam replied. "And I'm only going to answer the first one. Yes."

Three days later

AT FIRST SAM THOUGHT THAT BABBIT WOULD head for Aquilla, but it was soon obvious that he had another destination in mind. It was still south—Babbit hadn't changed his mind about going into Mexico, though there was always the possibility that he wouldn't even make it to the border. All the indications were that he was pushing his horse at a killing pace.

Sam, on the other hand, rode easily, sparingly, knowing that in the long run he would make just as good time because his horse would still be fresh while Babbit's horse was wearing out. On the third day Sam got close enough to get a glimpse of Babbit in the distance. That was when he knew the killer was heading for Puxico, another one of the little towns on the American side of the border.

Sam arrived in Puxico just about suppertime, and, along with the spicy aromas of Mexican cooking, he could smell coffee, pork chops, fried potatoes, and baking bread.

"Sasha? Sasha?" a woman called, and Sam, startled because that had been the name of the Indian girl Babbit had mutilated, jerked his horse to a halt to look in the direction of the call.

"Sí, signora?" a young, Mexican girl answered.

"Take the clothes down from the line, will you?" the woman ordered.

"Sí, signora," the servant girl replied.

The woman, startled by the fact that Sam had stopped his horse, looked at him nervously, and, instinctively, took a step backward. Sam touched the brim of his hat in greeting, then urged his horse on.

A game of checkers was being played by two gray-bearded men in front of the feed store, watched over by half a dozen kibitzers. A couple of them looked up at Sam as he rode by, his horse's hooves clumping hollowly on the hard-packed earth of the street. None of them seemed to recognize him, which was good, because Sam didn't exactly want his presence announced.

The shopkeeper who was running the dry-goods store came through his front door and began vigorously sweeping the wooden porch. His broom did little but raise the dust to swirl about, then fall back down again. He brushed a sleeping dog off the porch, but even before he went back inside, the dog reclaimed his position, curled around comfortably, and within a moment was asleep again.

Sam saw the horse from the far end of the street. As he had known from the trail, the animal had been ridden nearly to death, and even at a distance Sam could see that he was totally defeated.

Sam rode slowly down to the far end of the street, then tied his horse to a hitch rail next to the poor animal. He walked over to the horse and patted it on the neck. The horse's coat was smeared with foam and it was breathing in labored gasps. Its muzzle and the hitch rail were flecked with blood that had spewed from its mouth and nostrils by the painful breaths. It had been ridden until its lungs burst.

For a moment Sam felt a savage rage at a person who could do that to a horse.

Sam sighed, then pulled his pistol and aimed it at the horse's head. The horse looked toward him, his big brown eyes sad and knowing. He nodded once, almost as if telling Sam that he understood what had to be done. Then the horse looked away and waited stoically for the release from its suffering. Sam pulled the trigger and the horse fell to the ground. The gunshot echoed through the quiet streets for a long time. Then it was silent.

The gunshot attracted several of the townspeople. They looked toward the saloon, at the man with the smoking gun, and at the horse that lay motionless on the street.

A curtain fluttered in one of the false fronts.

A cat yowled somewhere down the street.

A fly buzzed past Sam's ear, did a few circles, then descended quickly to the horse, joined almost immediately by a dozen others, drawn to the unexpected feast.

Sam pushed through the bat-wing doors, then stepped to one side so that a wall was at his back. At the bar, a glass of beer in front of him, his lips dripping with moisture, stood Lucas Babbit.

Sam's lips twisted into an evil smile. Part of him wanted to kill the man this instant, while part of him wanted to delay the pleasure. He remembered the fear Charley Harris had shown toward hanging, and he wanted Babbit to know that same terror. Maybe he would take him back.

"Babbit," Sam said. His words were cold, flat, menacing.

Babbit didn't turn around, didn't even look at him in the mirror. Instead he stared into his glass of beer with those cold, droopy eyes.

"Well, look who's here. I would've thought you'd give up on me by now."

"I've come for you, Babbit."

There were half a dozen drinkers at the bar, and at Sam's words, they hurried to move away. Tables and chairs scooted across the floor as everyone in the saloon got up and moved back against the wall, out of the line of fire.

Sam caught the movement of the others out of the corner of his eye. He was pretty sure Babbit had not picked up any partners in his short flight of freedom, but he wanted to be certain. A quick glance was all it took to convince him that there was no one else who represented any danger to him.

Babbit still did not turn around. "What was that shooting out front?" he asked.

"I had to shoot your horse."

"You shouldn't have done that. That was a good horse."

"Not after you got through with him, you horse-killing son of a bitch."

"Well, he wasn't my horse anyway. I just borrowed him when I left," Babbit said with a low, evil laugh.

"You disappointed a few folks back there, Babbit. They were wanting to see you dance."

"I thought I'd just let old Charley do all the dancin' for me."

"Charley did his show. Now it's your turn."

"No, thank you. I got no plans to go hang."

"I don't give a damn what your plans are, Babbit. You're going back and you're going to hang."

"If you're so all-fired set on seein' me dead, Slater, why don't you just shoot me here and be done with it?"

"Huh-uh," Sam said. "Shooting you is too good for you. I saw the way Charley sweated before he was hung. I don't intend to deny myself the pleasure of seeing you go through the same thing."

Babbit turned away from the bar to look at Sam. He was smiling evilly.

"You know, Slater, I used to wonder why you kept on doggin' me when there was others with higher prices on their heads. Then someone told me that you took it real personal what me and Purdone did to that Injun girl. They said you know'd her. Is that right?"

"I knew her," Sam said.

"That's why you kept comin', huh?"

"That's why."

Babbit's evil smile spread. "Well, then, maybe I got somethin' here that'll square things up between us. Somethin' of the girl you can keep as a little memento." He started to reach into his vest pocket.

"Don't do it, Babbit!" Sam cautioned.

Babbit held out his hand. "Hey, now hold on there," he said. "I ain't goin' for no gun. Like I told you, all I'm reachin' for is a little memento." His hand came back out of his pocket, clutching a little piece of brown leather. "See?" He held it out toward Sam. "That there is for you. I'm givin' it to you."

"What is it?"

Babbit's evil grin grew wider. "I thought you said you knowed her, Slater. What's the matter? Didn't you ever see the girl's titties? This here is one of her tits. The left one."

"You sorry son of a bitch."

"Here, take it!" Babbit suddenly shouted, tossing it toward Sam.

Sam's first reaction was of revulsion, then he saw that Babbit was using this as a diversionary tactic, for in the same motion as the toss, his hand snaked down to his side to draw his pistol.

Sam reacted to the sudden move quickly, drawing his own pistol faster than he had ever drawn them before, spurred on in the effort by a year of controlled rage toward this man. He had his own gun out in time to take quick but deliberate aim and shoot Babbit in the gut. Babbit, the barrel of his own pistol just topping the holster, pulled the trigger, shooting lead into the floor. A red stain began to spread just over his belt buckle.

Babbit's gun clattered to the floor and he put his hands over his belly wound and watched the blood spill through his fingers. Inexplicably he smiled.

"You're fast, Slater," he said. "Faster'n I thought." He weaved back and forth for a moment, then pitched forward, crashing through a table before landing on the floor.

Smoke from the discharge of the weapons formed a big cloud, then began to drift toward the ceiling.

Sam knelt beside Babbit. The outlaw was still alive.

"This isn't how I wanted you to die, Babbit," he said. "I wanted to take you back. I wanted to see you hang."

Babbit tried to laugh, but it came out a barking cough. Little flecks of blood sprayed out onto his lips and his shirt.

"I reckon I beat you after all," he rasped. "I told you I wasn't goin' to hang."

"Not quite," Sam said. He stood up and rammed his pistol back in his holster. "Dead's dead, I reckon."

The bat-wings swung open and a man with a

badge came inside. His hair and mustache were gray, his face lined around his blue eyes. There was a sharpness to his eyes that told Sam the peace officer had probably been pretty good when he was younger. Only age had driven him to a backwater place like Puxico, where little happened. Age had undoubtedly slowed him down, but Sam imagined there were still a few who could make the mistake of misjudging him. Sam didn't intend to make that mistake.

"You shoot this fella?" the man with the badge asked.

"Yes," Sam answered.

"Want to tell me what it's all about?"

Babbit laughed, another coughing, blood-spraying laugh. "Sheriff, don't blame my friend here," he said. "If he hadn't killed me, I would have killed him. Fact is, he done me a favor. This way, at least, I ain't goin' to hang."

"That's right, Sheriff," one of the witnesses said. "The fella on the floor drew first. It was a pure case of self-defense."

"You shoulda seen it, Sheriff," another offered. "It was the fastest thing I ever seen in my life."

The sheriff sighed and looked at Sam. "Did you have to bring your beef to my town?"

"Sorry, Sheriff, but this is where I caught up with him," Sam said. He nodded toward Babbit. "This is Lucas Babbit. You'll find paper on him in your office. I'll be wantin' a receipt from you for him."

"You a bounty hunter?"

"Why, Sheriff, don't you recognize him?" Babbit asked. His voice was weaker now, and racked with pain. "This here is Sam Slater. Me and him is old friends now. He's been after me for more'n a year. He's the fella they call the Regulator."

The crowd reacted audibly to Babbit's announcement.

"The Regulator?" someone said.

"Slater?"

"I've heard of him."

"Boys we're goin' to have some story to tell. We just seen the Regulator in action," another said.

The sheriff held up his hand to silence the crowd reaction.

"I've heard of you, Slater," he said. "They say you're a hard man, but I've never heard tell of you shootin' one of your quarry in the back. All right, I'll give you your receipt, but then I want you to leave. If there's anything I don't want in this town, it's a gunfighter . . . even one that's on the side of the law. Do you get my drift?"

"I'll be on my way, Sheriff, soon as you give me the receipt," Sam said.

The sheriff went over to the bar. "Ed, you got a tablet and pencil?"

The bartender reached under the bar and came up with the items.

"Your name Lucas Babbit like he say?" the sheriff asked Babbit.

"That's it, Sheriff. Lucas Babbit, with two *b*'s," Babbit said. He snorted. "Wouldn't want my name misspelled on the tombstone."

"Received of Sam Slater, the body of one Lucas Babbit, wanted man, killed in a fair gunfight in the town of Puxico. Signed, Sheriff Emil Dobbins," the sheriff said, speaking aloud as he wrote. He tore the page off the tablet and handed it to Sam. "Will that do you?"

"That will do just fine, Sheriff. Thank you," Sam answered, folding the piece of paper and putting it in his shirt pocket. He started toward the door.

"Slater, wait a minute!" Babbit called to Sam. "You ain't goin' to just leave me like this, are you? I got a pain in my gut somethin' awful. Why didn't you shoot me in the head or the heart and get it over with?"

"I shot you just where I wanted to shoot you, Babbit," Sam said.

"Well, finish me off now, you bastard!" Babbit shouted. "Don't you leave me like this!"

Sam started for the door again.

"Slater! Slater, don't forget the girl's tit!" Babbit called. "You wouldn't want to leave her tittie behind for someone else to play with, would you?"

Sam stopped.

"Yeah!" Babbit said. "Yeah, think about that tit. You don't want to leave it, do you?"

Sam remained rooted to the floor, though his hand began to move slowly toward his pistol.

"That's it!" Babbit said. "That's it! Shoot me! Yes, go ahead! Shoot me!"

Sam sighed and let his arm drop down to his side. He started once more toward the door.

"Don't you want me to die? What's the matter? Are you showing yellow?"

Sam pushed through the bat-wing doors, walked by Babbit's dead horse, and climbed on his own animal for the long ride back to Gunther. After more than a year of burning, the fire in his gut was out.